Genna Ross had finally come home . . .

She lay back against the rock and sobbed as the past pulled at her heartstrings.

What had the Psalmist said? "I lift up my eyes to the hills — where does my help come from? My help comes from the Lord, the Maker of heaven and earth."

As much as she loved the hills, she knew that they were temporal things and no strength could be gained from them. She'd long known that only God could supply her needs, but she'd allowed herself to lose contact with Him

A sound behind her startled Genna out of her reverie and she turned quickly, swiping at her eyes.

Evan Sullivan looked at her reproachfully. "So it was you. Why did you lie to me?"

"I don't remember our conversation exactly, but I don't believe I lied. I am Genna Ross now."

IRENE B. BRAND is an award-winning inspirational romance novelist who has written ten novels and articles for numerous historical and religious periodicals. A retired teacher, Mrs. Brand resides in West Virginia when she isn't pursuing her other active pastime, international travel.

Books by Irene B. Brand

ROMANCE READER—TWO BOOKS IN ONE

RR2—A Change in Heart & A Mighty Flame

Heartstrings

Irene B. Brand

Heartsong Presents

ISBN 1-55748-332-9

HEARTSTRINGS

PRINTED IN U.S.A.

one

From her vantage point on Pinnacle Rock, Veevie Wooten saw Evan Sullivan as he parked his truck at the base of the mountain. Steadily climbing, it would take Evan half an hour to reach her. Relaxed, Veevie leaned against the gnarled oak tree that through the centuries had forced its way through the rocky base to wrap strong tentacles around the cliff.

The sun shone unseasonably warm for mid-October and Veevie cast her sweater aside. Appalachia had its faults but from this spot it was hard to find them. A dense, almost unbroken forest cover blanketed the rugged landscape. Wispy haze lent mystery to the colorful hills swaddled in the yellow, red, and brown leaves of autumn. Sun filtered through the branches of the old oak, and the girl arched her back to take full advantage of the warm rays that turned her auburn hair into a kaleidoscope of burnished hues.

"Wish I had a dollar for every time I've looked at that old mountain," she murmured aloud. "Sixteen years of seein' the same view, and I ain't tired of hit yet."

Veevie refrained from glancing to her left. She knew what she'd see if she looked that way. *A naked mountain, that's what it is*, she thought, and she shook her head in disgust.

"Shameful people, to tear away the mountains for

a handful of coal," she muttered.

Her thoughts echoed Grandpap's sentiments, but how could she help it? She'd always lived with him.

Veevie scanned the length of the Mill Creek Valley that snaked its way between two high mountain ranges. Dilapidated buildings of the Miller coal mine remained at the head of the hollow where two streams tumbled down the mountainside to form Mill Creek. A lake that had formed behind tons of mine debris sparkled in the sunshine. At the mouth of the creek, a few buildings of the Sullivan No. 2 mine protruded above the treetops.

Until a few years ago, scores of miners had lived in the valley, but when the Miller mine closed, they'd moved on to other towns. Grandpap had bought his house from the coal company, as had a few other miners, but Mill Creek now had less than fifty residents along its eight-mile journey to the Guyandotte River.

Evan's step startled her. He climbed the ledge to sit beside her. "What a sour face! Aren't you glad to see me?"

She moved close to him. Veevie hadn't seen him since the first of September when he'd gone away to college, and she yearned to feel his arms around her.

"Hit's been long, Evan. I've missed you." She fondled his curly brown hair and blended into his arms. Without looking, Veevie could feel Evan's ever-present smile, one that crinkled his gray eyes and lit up his strong features. She'd missed Evan's smile most of all, or at least she thought that was what she'd missed until he lowered his lips to hers.

Veevie squirmed in his embrace as Evan's lips traced a path to her ear lobe.

"I've missed you, too, Veevie. Happy sixteenth birthday."

"I was afeared you wouldn't come, Evan."

"I promised, didn't I?" he said, with a slight frown, and Veevie wondered what she'd done to vex him.

He drew a small box from his pocket.

"Oh, Evan, you didn't need to bring no present. Just havin' you is all the birthday I want."

But she took the box with eager fingers. "Oh," she gasped when she saw the ring.

"It's an opal. That's the October birthstone." When tears clouded her green eyes, he continued, "It's not an expensive ring since I don't have much money now. But one of these days I'll buy you lots of jewelry. Until then, that ring will be a reminder that you belong to me."

His lips cut off her words of thanks, but Veevie soon broke their embrace. "Hit's purty, Evan. I'll keep hit always. How long will we have to wait?"

"Too long," he whispered. "My father has big plans for me, and marriage isn't one of them."

A hawk soared high above them, screeching its displeasure at a flock of blackbirds chattering among the trees. Wispy clouds floated across the blue sky. The sun's heat radiating from the rock made Veevie drowsy.

Her contentment fled at Evan's next words. "I have bad news for us, Veevie."

She roused, frightened. "What?"

"Dad has decided that I need to change schools. I'll be leaving the state university at midterm. I've been accepted by the engineering school at the University of California at Berkeley. I'm going there in January and Dad wants me to continue through the summer."

"So you won't be workin' at the mine next year?"

"No, he thinks I've had enough on-the-job experience. The other things I need to know are in books, he says."

"But, Evan, don't you ever think for yourself? You're almost twenty years old. Shouldn't you make some decisions on your own?" She knew she had no right to question, but the fact that he was leaving scared her. *Had his father found about about her*?

"Dad doesn't force me into anything. I want to learn all I can about mining—after all, I'll be managing the company someday. It will be only a few more years."

"Morgantown was far enough away. Hard to tell when I'll see you again."

He lifted her hand and kissed it. "Oh, I'll be home sometimes on vacations. Logan County isn't so far from Charleston. I'll see you as often as I can." He put his arm around her. "You know I've loved you for over a year. I'm not going to change. We can't be married until I'm through college, but do we have to wait for everything?"

"Yes, we do," she said, and her voice trembled. "I've told you before that I won't shame Grandpap like my ma done. It's bad enough that he's had me on his hands—I ain't takin' no chance of givin' him another kid to raise." She looked at him, and her voice mirrored the pleading in her sea-green eyes. "Please, Evan, don't ask me. I ain't strong enough to hold out against you forever. Don't ask me no more."

He sighed guiltily and looked away.

"All right, Veevie. I guess I respect you more for saying no."

"I'm glad somebody respects me. Not many folks do. Hit's all right to buy liquor from the local moonshiner, but decent folks won't get too chummy with his granddaughter." She tried not to sound bitter but the look of compassion on Evan's face told her she hadn't succeeded.

"It has never made any difference to me, Veevie. You know that."

"I know, Evan, you've never shunned me, and that's why hit's hard to deny you anything."

Evan looked away from her across the mountain and she followed his gaze. Without glancing her way, he said, "Veevie, as my wife, you'll live in the city and meet lots of important people. Why don't you start grooming yourself for that? And can't you learn to speak the English language correctly? You shouldn't say 'hit', and 'ain't'—you know better."

"Hit's the way I've talked all of my life."

"Is there any reason you can't change? For me?"

"You're ashamed of me, ain't you, Evan?" *Why hadn't she realized that before*? He'd never wanted to see her out in public. She'd met Evan last summer when he'd come to Logan County to work in the new mine his father had opened at the mouth of the hollow. They'd seen each other often, but all of their meetings had either been here on the pinnacle or at her home.

"No, I'm not ashamed of you."

Veevie's day was ruined, and she slid off the rock and started down the path.

"I didn't want to hurt you, Veevie, but if you come out in my world talking as you do now, you're going to be hurt a lot more."

Veevie thought that instant she'd return his ring, but she had to have some remembrance of him. He tagged behind her down the narrow path until they reached his truck.

"You're angry with me now, Veevie, but you think about what I said. You're a smart girl, and there's no need for you to bury yourself in these mountains. Plan to go to college as soon as you finish high school."

Veevie couldn't answer him. It seemed as if a giant hand had clamped around her throat. She wanted to hurl angry words at him. "Maybe I don't want to be in your world," her mind thundered, but her rebellious heart whispered, "Oh, yes, you do. Admit it, life without Evan will be pointless."

She woodenly received his kiss. "Wear the ring, my little sweetheart. Let it remind you that I love you. I'll be back someday, and we'll meet on Pinnacle Rock."

Like a wild deer, she darted away from him and into the woods. She couldn't watch him leave for in her heart she believed she'd never see him again.

Her heartstrings, which had seemed so full and vibrant a few hours ago, were now tuned to the breaking point.

Veevie heard shouting when she entered the clearing and she rounded the corner of the cabin on a run. Grandpap stood on the porch, a leveled shotgun in his hands.

"I ain't sellin' my land to no strippin' company," he thundered. "Get off my property."

"Now be reasonable, Mr. Wooten," the man at the foot of the steps pleaded. "We've an option to buy much of the other land in this valley, but your property is the key to the whole area."

Veevie ran to the man, grabbed him by the arm, and propelled him toward the truck standing beside the road.

"There ain't no reasonin' with Grandpap when he's holdin' a shotgun, Mister Man. I don't know what you've said to rile him, but you'd best be gettin' away from here."

The man shrugged his shoulders in defeat, mumbling, "There's nothing on earth more cantankerous than an ignorant mountaineer."

The engine of the pickup roared as the man raced recklessly down the dirt road.

Veevie followed John Wooten into the log cabin and watched as he placed the gun on a rack above the mantle. He gasped for breath and lowered his body weakly into a rocker by the fireplace. In his youth Grandpap had been tall and brawny, but sickness had taken its toll and he was only a shadow of the man who'd cared for her when she was a child.

"Grandpap, you ought not to get upset like that. What was the ruckus about?"

The old man spat contemptuously into the open fireplace. "That skunk works for a company that's tryin' to buy up land in Logan County. I ain't sellin' no mineral rights to 'em."

Fortunately, Evan's father operated deep mines; otherwise, Grandpap would never have let him come to see her. Grandpap had been a coal miner for years until black lung disease had forced his retirement, but he'd always hated strip mining and what it was doing to the mountaintops of West Virginia.

"And don't you sell to 'em when I'm dead and gone neither," he hurled at Veevie.

"I won't, Grandpap, but don't talk about dyin'."

"We've got to talk about hit, and I aim to do that in a little bit, soon's as I get my breath. Why didn't Evan come by?"

She refused to meet his eyes and busied herself sweeping the ashes off the hearth.

"Didn't he show up?"

"Yes, he came, but I don't think he'll be back. He's ashamed of me."

"Did he say so?" Grandpap shouted in a voice still strong in spite of black lung.

"No, of course not." She wouldn't let Grandpap bad-mouth Evan even if she were mad at him. "But why wouldn't he be ashamed of me? Look at me."

"I've been a-watchin' you grow up for sixteen years, and you're a right purty girl in my book."

"Maybe, until I open my mouth." Veevie had never smiled much because she wanted to keep her crooked teeth covered. That had been bad enough, but now she realized that her speech was as ugly as her teeth.

"You want to get your teeth fixed? Ain't there braces or such that will straighten 'em? All you have to do is ask me. I've got some money."

"Moonshine money!" Veevie said bitterly.

"I've got money that didn't come from my still. All I've made from the liquor I added to my black lung pension to keep food on the table. I don't keep anything from hit."

He motioned her to a chair beside him. The house was too hot for Veevie but Grandpap needed the added warmth.

"Hit's time we had a little talk, girl. I ain't goin' to live much longer, and I want you to know what's what."

She started to protest, and he held up his hand. "Don't argue. You've got to face facts. Black lung works slow, but hit's a relentless foe. I want you to know how I've provided for your future."

He chewed slowly on his tobacco and spat into the fire.

"I've been layin' aside a nice little nest egg in the bank at Logan, and I've got a lawyer down there takin' care of my money. Hit all goes to you when I'm dead." Grandpap paused to catch his breath. "Last summer, when Cousin Bea was visitin' from California, I asked her if you could come and live with her when I die. She's a refined woman and can shape you up where you lack manners and right talkin'. There'll be plenty of money for college if you want to go."

"But that means I'd have to leave the mountains!"

"Hit'll be best for you to leave here and make somethin' of yourself where nobody's ever heard of the Wootens. I want your promise—will you do hit?"

She nodded slowly but her heart would not consent.

"As far as that's concerned, you'll still have this place. Your money'll be in a trust fund, and I've made arrangements that the taxes will be paid on this land until you get yourself settled. Hit'll always be here so you can come if you want to, but I don't want you tied to the place. After a few years, you can do what you want to with hit, but I'm hopin' you won't sell hit to no coal company that'll strip the land."

"I promise to do what you want me to, Grandpap."

He ruffled her hair, as near as he ever came to affection. "All right, that's enough of this funeral palaver. Let's go talk to Ivy about gettin' your teeth fixed."

John Wooten's cousin, Ivy Fisher, and her husband Ben lived a mile away but Veevie had to hustle to keep up with Grandpap's long-legged gait.

"You talk about dyin' and then outwalk me. You're good for a long time."

John stubbornly shook his head but said nothing. When they reached the Fishers' ramshackle abode John explained to Ivy the reason for the visit.

"There's a man in Logan can do hit, and Ben can drive her in tomorrow to see about hit," said Ivy.

As John sauntered out to the potato patch to see

Ben, Ivy called to him, "I'm fixin' supper for you, so don't figure on rushin' back up the creek."

When John was out of hearing, Ivy turned to Veevie. "What's brought on this sudden fit to have your teeth fixed?"

Ivy Fisher, in her midfifties, had wiry silver hair that crowned an angular face with chin and jaws sharp enough to cut paper. Veins were prominent in her thin neck. What Ivy lacked in beauty she made up for in a personality that was pleasant and outgoing. She mothered both Veevie and John, and Veevie often brought her problems to the older woman.

"Evan hurt my feelings, and I let Grandpap find out about hit. He thinks fixin' my teeth will make me feel better, but that won't heal the hurt that Evan is ashamed of me."

"Hit's never a good idea to marry up, Veevie. I feared you were headed for a fall when you started courtin' Evan. Mine owners and miners just don't mix."

Veevie had heard that all her life, but she'd thought that she and Evan could overcome the barrier.

Before she could answer, a knock sounded at the door.

"Come in," Ivy called, and Miss Amelia Dixon entered.

"Pardon my laziness, Miss Amelia. I didn't know hit was you, or I'd have come to the door," Ivy apologized.

"No matter," Miss Amelia said as she smoothed back the iron gray hair from her face. Ivy scurried out of her chair and urged the short, lean woman toward the best seat in the room. As a missionary, Miss Amelia had become a fixture along the creek during the past ten years as she worked with the children, visited in troubled homes, and helped the elderly. She seemed to have an unusual knack of knowing when trouble came. Had she divined that Veevie was downhearted today? Veevie thought her romance with Evan had remained a secret, so she doubted if Miss Amelia even knew of Evan's attentions.

It appeared Miss Amelia had only wanted to talk to Ivy, but when she left the Fisher household, she asked Veevie to walk to the car with her.

"I've been missing you at church, Veevie. Has your faith faltered?"

"No, I don't think so," Veevie said, "but sometimes my family background stands in the way. I often think hit's better for the other kids if I stay away. I'm an embarrassment to them."

"Don't be foolish, Veevie! That's your imagination—the youth at the church have been kind to you."

Kind to me, but they've never accepted me for what I am, Veevie thought, but she didn't want to hurt Miss Amelia, so she said nothing.

"I want you to come back on Sunday," Miss Amelia insisted.

"All right, I'll plan to come. Thanks for bein' concerned about me."

"God is concerned about you, too, Veevie. Remember His words, 'The Spirit itself beareth witness with our spirit, that we are the children of God:

And if children, then heirs; heirs of God, and joint-heirs with Christ.' I can understand why you're self-conscious about the circumstances of your birth, but that shouldn't stand in the way of your spiritual growth. If you're a child of God, your natural birth doesn't matter. I'm expecting great things of you, Veevie."

"I'm glad your grandfather lived to see you graduate from high school," Bea said. The cabin hadn't yet lost its funeral smell from the flowers the neighbors had brought to Grandpap's wake, and the sight of his emaciated body lying in the coffin still haunted Veevie.

Listlessly she helped her cousin close the house. She didn't want to leave home, but she'd promised her dying grandfather more than once that she'd go to California with Bea. Veevie knew she could get a job and support herself here, but before he died, Grandpap had made her promise again. "Go to Bea's for a while. See somethin' of the world. There's a lot more to life than you'll ever find in Logan County."

Veevie closed her suitcase and stood for a moment looking around the cabin. Cousin Bea had agreed with her that it was best to leave the house as it was while Grandpap had lived. Ivy and Ben had promised to look after the place for her.

"I want to walk around a little, Cousin Bea."

"Don't be too long. We should arrive in Charleston before dark. Our plane leaves Yeager Airport at nine o'clock in the morning."

"I won't be gone more than an hour or two. I want

to say goodbye to a few places."

After a brisk climb, Veevie stood on Pinnacle Rock and glanced out over the creek valley. She hadn't seen or heard from Evan for over two years, but when she stood here on their rock, she felt as close to him as if he held her in his arms. Just one small note after he went away to college in California, and that was it.

For two years she'd devoted every thought and act to becoming the woman he wanted her to be. She had excelled in her school classes and had spent hours with the missionary learning proper conduct. This contact with Miss Amelia had also introduced Veevie to an inner spiritual strength that saw her safely through days of prejudice at school and the trying hours of Grandpap's slow death. She had made her life over for Evan, but he apparently didn't care anymore. She had hoped he'd read about Grandpap's passing and would come to comfort her, but she'd looked for him in vain.

Admit it, Veevie! Admit the reason you don't want to leave here is because you keep hoping he'll come back to you. Could she leave Appalachia without trying to see him once more? Veevie pondered the question as she hurried down the mountain.

Veevie and Bea arrived in Charleston by midafternoon. When they entered the motel room, Veevie still hadn't decided what she should do. She twirled the opal ring on her finger, watching the rainbow hues catch the sunlight. She hadn't removed it since the day Evan had placed it there. When Bea went into the bathroom, Veevie found a telephone directory in the nightstand and her finger hovered over the names until she found Sullivan Mining Company.

She lifted the receiver. She didn't even know whether Evan had come home or if he were still away at school.

She dialed the number rapidly before Bea returned. "I want to speak to Evan Sullivan, please," she said with bated breath when the receptionist answered.

"Mr. Sullivan is on another line at the moment. May I take a message?"

As Bea was opening the bathroom door Veevie replaced the phone receiver.

I have to see him, she thought desperately.

"Cousin Bea," Veevie said. "There's an old friend of mine here in Charleston I want to contact. Do you mind if I leave for a little while?"

"No, go ahead, I want to rest anyway. Do you want to take the car? I won't turn it in until we reach the airport."

"No, thanks. The office is on Kanawha Boulevard, just a few blocks from here, I think. I'll ask directions, and if it's too far to walk, I'll take a taxi."

Having funds was still a novelty to Veevie. *Grandpap hadn't been funning when he said he'd accumulated a nest egg for her*, she mused. He'd left plenty of money to make her independent so she could pay her way with Cousin Bea.

The motel clerk directed Veevie to the Sullivan Mining Company and she walked quickly along the street until she came to the stone building fronting on the Kanawha River. Her steps slowed as she entered the imposing edifice and the movement of the elevator made her stomach churn as the cage lifted rapidly to the sixth floor. She checked the doors until she found one marked, "Evan Sullivan, Vice-President."

Taking a deep breath, she gingerly opened the heavy door. Veevie expelled the breath that she didn't even know she was holding when she entered the reception room. The blond secretary looked up expectantly.

"I'd like to see Mr. Sullivan, please, Mr. Evan Sullivan."

The woman looked at the book in front of her. "Do you have an appointment?"

Veevie shook her head.

"Mr. Sullivan is a busy man and he rarely sees anyone without an appointment."

Veevie's thoughts exploded inside her. *I have to see him. After coming this far, I have to see him. If she won't let me go in, I'll jump over her desk and rush through his door.*

"I want to talk to him," she demanded, staring at the woman, although her heart hammered in her chest.

The secretary said haughtily, "May I have your name and the nature of your business with him?"

"Tell him Genevieve Wooten would like a few minutes of his time."

The woman pushed a button on the intercom.

"Yes?" Evan's voice sounded in the room, and Veevie held on to the desk to steady herself.

"A Genevieve Wooten is here to see you, sir."

Did he hesitate? It seemed so to Veevie, and her heart skipped a few beats before he answered, "Certainly. Send her in."

Veevie's hand shook so much she could hardly open the door. Evan stood to greet her. "This is quite a surprise, Veevie. Please sit down."

Fortunately, a heavy walnut desk separated them or she'd have run into his arms. For a moment his presence overwhelmed her to silence, then she whispered, "You've changed so much, Evan. I hardly know you."

His curly hair was the same, as were his gray eyes, but a close-cropped beard made him look much older, more mature, more unattainable.

His smile was as ready as always. "You've changed quite a lot yourself. What brings you to Charleston?"

Oh, Evan, have you forgotten everything? *Didn't your promise mean anything*?

She lifted her hand to the desktop, hoping he'd see the opal ring and remember, but her hand stopped suddenly when she saw the smiling portrait of the woman in a gilded frame. Veevie stared at the picture and then shifted her eyes to Evan who refused to meet her gaze.

The telephone rang but Evan didn't answer it. The intercom buzzed and the secretary's voice sounded, "Your wife is on the phone, Mr. Sullivan. She wants to know what time you'll be home for dinner."

Veevie scrambled to her feet and bolted from his office, not heeding his repeated calls to come back.

two

The driver braked suddenly when he saw the S-curve warning sign, and the occupants of the huge bus slid sideways in their seats. Lounging in her private compartment at the rear of the bus, Genna Ross seemed unperturbed by the dangers of the narrow, winding road. She laughed at the expression on the face of her manager, Jim Slater.

"Relax, Jim. People drive over these roads every day."

The bus careened wildly, and Jim grabbed a book to keep it from falling off the table. Jim was a slender man of thirty-five, and the expensive cut of his tailored suit showed off his well-knit physique. His neatly trimmed blond hair and full beard emphasized the blue of his eyes.

"Whatever possessed you to accept an engagement in such a Godforsaken place is more than I can imagine. Why didn't you let me check into the details first? After all, it's my job to manage your affairs. And to think you're doing this as a benefit!"

"Jim, did you ever see anyone die from black lung disease?"

"No," he answered carelessly.

"Well, I have, and it's not an easy death. That's the reason I'm giving a concert for miners with the disease. And remember, it is *my* affair."

As Genna looked out the window she realized she wasn't as calm as she appeared. How many people would identify country singing star Genna Ross as Logan County's own Veevie Wooten? Ten years had seen many changes: A new hair color, expert grooming, and the weariness of fame had changed the wildflower into a greenhouse orchid. *Would anyone recognize her*? Surely not Evan Sullivan, should she be unfortunate enough to encounter him.

She had refused an invitation to sing at the Civic Center in Charleston, much to Jim's displeasure, simply because of Evan. But in spite of the pain it might cause her, she longed to return to Logan County, and the invitation had presented too great a temptation. The chances of seeing Evan in the small town where she'd attended high school were slim.

"And why are you taking two weeks off after the concert without telling me where you're going?"

"Quit crabbing, Jim! Look on it as a bonus. You only had to reschedule three engagements and you receive two weeks' vacation in the bargain."

"But why be so secretive about what you're going to do?"

"There are times when I'd like to forget that I'm Genna Ross, when I just want to be myself. I can't do that if you're following me around trying to make me famous."

"That's not the real reason I want to be around you, Genna. You keep leading me on but you never let me come too close."

Genna's green eyes glittered angrily, and she clamped her mouth on an angry retort. Swallowing once, she said calmly, "Be fair, Jim. I've never led you on, never once have I given you any reason to believe you're anything except a manager to me. I hope we've become friends, but it will be nothing else. You must make up your mind to that."

Jim picked up her latest album lying on the table between them. " 'A One-Man Woman,' " he read the title song. "That song made you rich. Why can't I be that one man? I've wanted you long enough, and you don't seem to want anyone else. Are you in love with somebody—is there some lost love you're yearning for?"

Genna didn't want to quarrel with Jim but she didn't like his prying. Now that she'd achieved fame, she couldn't hide her Logan County background much longer. Not that she was ashamed of her youth, but thinking about home always brought back Evan's memory. Why couldn't she forget him? At least if this visit unearthed her past, no one would ever know about Evan, since for his own reasons, he'd kept their meetings secret.

"Jim, I've appreciated all the things you've done for me, but as far as I'm concerned, the time has come for us to go separate ways. I'm willing for you to leave whenever you want to."

His face paled at first, then broke into an angry frown. "Are you really serious? Don't you realize that I've made you a star?"

Genna laughed. "Oh, is it your voice and body

that fans come to hear and see? Excuse me, I thought it was mine."

"Joke about it all you like, Genna, but our lives are too closely entwined to consider separation. I didn't intend to make you mad, but I don't like the idea of being told I'm fired."

"I'm willing to forget it if you are, on the condition that you realize I'm the one who makes the final decision on everything. You don't own me or my career, Jim. Remember that."

Not giving Jim a chance to reply, Genna moved out of the room toward the front of the bus. Cary Mullins chatted with the driver. The three band members slumbered in their seats. Lori Blair, Genna's secretary, pored over the latest issue of *Country Lanes*.

" 'One-Man Woman' is still on the Top 10, Genna. Congratulations!"

Genna nodded her thanks and went to sit beside Cary who had been with Genna for five years as her makeup artist, hair stylist, and masseuse. Cary had become, however, much more valuable than her job description. Of all the people in her employ, Genna had the greatest regard for this woman.

Cary gave her employer an understanding smile and gently massaged the muscles of Genna's neck. Like a kitten being stroked, her long slender body relaxed under Cary's skillful hands.

"Ah, Cary," she sighed contentedly, "what would I do without you?"

"Jim been badgering you again?" the stocky

African-American woman asked.

"Uh-huh. The pressure of these tours is bad enough without having constant company. I have half a notion to sell this bus and travel by plane. Too much togetherness isn't good for us."

Jim strode down the aisle and sat on the seat opposite her.

"I've been talking to the editor of one of the state's major newspapers. He'll be at that high school for an interview at seven o'clock, so you'll need to have her ready by then, Cary."

Genna's muscles tightened under Cary's hands.

"No interview, Jim. I'm here to give the benefit show, but I don't have any other obligation to the town. It isn't as if they were doing me a favor."

"But. . . ," Jim began.

"Call and cancel the interview. I'm tired, and a two-hour show is all I'm going to do tonight. Cary, please order food brought to the motel after the show. We'll eat together."

Jim stomped angrily down the aisle, and Cary lowered an eyelid at Genna as Lori followed him.

"Going to sympathize with him, I suppose. I wish the two of them would make a match of it. Then maybe he'd leave you alone."

"She's willing, but he isn't," Genna answered. "It takes two to make a match, Grandpap always said. Most of the time I don't pay any attention to Jim. Guess I'm just irritable today."

Coming home shouldn't have made her irritable, but ten years was a long time, and she couldn't help worry about what this return might do to her career. She hoped her fame was strong enough that her public wouldn't mind if they found out that she'd been the illegitimate granddaughter of the local moonshiner. That didn't bother her as much, however, as the possibility of resurrecting memories of Evan. After all these years, she could still close her eyes, feel the sensation of his lips on hers, and revel in the closeness of his embrace. Genna had planned this homecoming as a sort of catharsis. If he'd cast a spell on her, maybe a visit to old surroundings would expunge it. *But what would happen if she saw him*?

When they entered Logan County Genna strained her eyes to see Pinnacle Rock but unshed tears clouded her vision. She almost cried again when they entered the small town of Woodville where she'd attended high school. Many of the stores were closed and vacant company houses loomed on the hills. The whole place had a neglected look. Genna had heard that mine mechanization had meant a loss of jobs for miners and that the population had decreased accordingly.

The manager of the motel rushed out to meet them and showed Genna to what was obviously the best room in the building.

"We're delighted to have you, Miss Ross. Not many people of your fame would take time for us. Anything I can do for you, let me know."

"My friend, Cary, will want a room that adjoins mine, and she'll be ordering food for us. Otherwise, I'd like not to be disturbed to allow time for me to rest before the concert."

Jim followed Genna into the room and looked disgustedly at the faded draperies, the none-too-clean carpet, and the meager furnishings. He turned on the manager but Genna headed him off.

"I'll be very comfortable here, sir. I appreciate your hospitality."

After the manager left, Jim angrily poked his fingers into the lumpy bed. "This is nothing but a hovel."

"I've slept in worse places, and it wouldn't have helped my popularity if you'd thrown a fit about the room. He's offering the best he has."

"I'm going to sleep on the bus."

"Help yourself. That will save me some money for your lodging." Cary laughed when Jim exited angrily and slammed the door.

"I'm glad you don't allow him to run over you, Genna. He's getting too big for his britches, as the old saying goes."

Genna soaked in a tub of hot water then relaxed under a massage from Cary. She slipped into pink slacks and a matching floral blouse for the ride to the auditorium. Her stage garments would be at the schoolhouse. The chauffeur, Lance, waited at the door of the motel with her Mercedes.

"Thanks for bringing the car, Lance," Genna said as she and Cary settled into the back seat. "I want to use it for a few days' vacation. You can travel back to Nashville on the bus, but I suppose Jim told you that."

Easing the car away from the motel, Lance said, "He told me. I'll be glad to drive you around on a trip if you like, Miss Genna."

"Thanks, guy, but I want you to have some free time too. Why, are you afraid I'll wreck the car?"

He grinned. "No chance of that; I've seen you drive. I sometimes wonder why you need me."

"She wants you for a bodyguard, you big hunk," Cary assured him.

"She may need one tonight. Lots of people are ganging into that little auditorium." He wheeled the white Mercedes into a small lot behind the building and parked at the same spot the school bus had stopped years ago to unload its passengers. Passing through the door into the hallway behind the stage, Genna marveled to herself, the place even smells the same. *I feel as if I've been transported back into time. I'll bet if the bell would ring, I'd dart into Room 55 for my English class.*

Jim cut short Genna's musings when he hurried toward her. "You have thirty minutes before the first show starts."

Genna dressed in sequined mauve pants and a matching silk blouse and sat on a dressing stool so that Cary could style her hair and apply her face. Observing her image in the mirror, Genna thought there was little chance that any former classmates would recognize her. Heavy shadow made her sea-green eyes appear dark and sultry, and not since her rise to stardom had the natural auburn hair appeared. Cary worked diligently to keep Genna's hair in the honey-blond tones her fans loved.

Because she'd lived so long with Bea in California, the news writers had yet to piece together her ragged past. *Give them time*, she thought, but at least her physical appearance wouldn't give her secret away. Before she returned to the circuit, she intended to visit Grandpap's old house and find her graduation picture to compare the changes time had made.

Genna stood offstage and listened to Jim launch into his flowery introduction. Genna seldom suffered stage fright, but tonight she felt a slight quickening of her pulse. If she only knew who would be in that audience, she'd feel better.

She raced onstage, blowing kisses to the crowd and waving to them. A sea of faces greeted her, and as their adulation soared around her, she thought of the time she'd tried out for the senior class play, and was turned down. A part in that play would have meant much more than all of their cheers tonight.

Forcibly, she pushed the past aside, signaled her band, and launched into the show as she would have in any other place.

I'm a one-man woman
From morning till night,
In the dark times of life
His love brings me light.
And if he will open his heart's closed door
I'll be a one-man woman forevermore.

That song had become her trademark in the past six months. She tried to believe that she didn't have Evan in mind when she wrote the lyrics, but here in these old surroundings she admitted she still loved him as much as she once had. With pathos marking her words, she sang:

No other man will claim me for life,
No other man can make me his wife,
Only one man will win my heart . . .
For I've been a one-man woman right from the start.

It didn't help to remind herself that Evan already had a wife. That fact was etched indelibly in her soul and mind.

During the intermission Genna mingled with the crowd, signing programs and shaking hands. No one showed any sign of recognition, nor did she meet anyone who seemed familiar to her. Hordes of people still waited to shake her hand when Jim propelled her toward the dressing room. She took five minutes to drink a cup of hot tea and change into another garment.

Cary had a blue gingham pioneer dress and a matching bonnet ready for her to wear. She tied the string loosely to let the bonnet dangle over Genna's shoulders. Onstage again, Genna sat on a high stool and reached for a dulcimer. The beginning of her last act always featured mountain folk songs that she'd learned from Grandpap and his neighbors. Tonight as she sang these simple, well-loved tunes she hoped her audience would be pleased.

Poor little turtle dove, setting on a pine,
Longing for his own true love as I did once
for mine,
For mine, as I did once for mine.

The applause convinced Genna that she'd chosen well, and she continued her repertoire, ending with the ballad that Evan had loved because it reminded him of Scotland, his ancestral home.

A bonnie, wee lassie whose name it was Nell,
Lived in a house where her grandmother
dwelled.
The house it was small, and the windows
no less,
Having four panes, one needed a glass,
That nice little window, the cute little
window,
The sweet little window where grand-
mother dwelled.

After she answered her second curtain call, Genna ran offstage where Cary waited with a lightweight coat. They hustled down to Lance and the waiting car and were gone before the crowd began to leave the building. Jim and Lori would supervise the band as they packed up the equipment and stored it on the bus.

"Oh, but I'm tired, Cary. I must be getting old. These engagements exhaust me."

"You put so much of yourself into it. I watched from the wings, and you've never done so well.

Seemed as if a new Genna was out there on the stage."

"Or an old Genna," she murmured.

The next morning Genna waved to her crew as they pulled out of the parking lot. She slid behind the wheel of the Mercedes and followed them for several miles. She hoped to give the appearance that she was traveling with the bus. She didn't want any fans following her, nor did she want Jim and Lori to have a clue to what she planned to do during her self-imposed leave. She spent the morning driving around the area seeing old places. When she went by the Sullivan No. 1 mine, she was surprised to see that it was closed. Most of the company houses were boarded up, and the company store, while still in operation, had few customers. In her childhood the store had always been crowded. She looked in dismay at the strip mines in the area. When she came to the crossroads that led to her childhood home on Mill Creek, she turned the car back toward the town of Logan. Too many memories in one day was more than she could handle.

She registered for a motel room under the name Genevieve Wooten and telephoned Ivy and Ben. Overjoyed to know she was in town, they would be glad to have her stay with them for a few days.

"Thanks, but if the old house is still livable, I'll hang around there."

"We've kept it just like when you were here, Veevie. You'll feel right at home," Ivy assured her.

She telephoned the attorney who handled all of

her affairs in Logan County and made an appointment to see him the next day. When hunger pains made Genna realize that she hadn't eaten since breakfast, she left the motel to look for a cafe. It had been years since she'd had to think about her personal needs.

"I'll starve to death without Jim and Cary to wait on me," she said to no one in particular.

Leaving the restaurant, Genna paused with her hand on the car door. She heard heavy footsteps behind her and a sudden silence as if someone had stopped closeby.

"Veevie?"

Genna gripped the side of the car for a moment, but she ignored the voice and slipped under the steering wheel, keeping her back to the speaker. She didn't have to look to know it was Evan.

He stepped closer to the car.

"Veevie?" he said again, and she steeled herself to look at him.

"Are you speaking to me?" she said, without a hint of an Appalachian accent. Her speech teacher at college had made sure of that. "My name is Genna."

She could tell by the expression on his face that she had almost convinced him he'd made a mistake. Almost, but not quite.

"I'm sorry," he said slowly. "I thought you were a friend I'd been expecting to come back to Logan County someday. Your walk and posture resembled hers, but I can see now that you don't look like her."

"Sorry to disappoint you," Genna said as she started the car's engine. She had to escape his piercing gaze.

"Did you say your name was Genna?" Evan asked, apparently reluctant to have her leave.

Genna nodded.

"Genna Ross, by any chance?"

Genna hesitated, but nodded again. She couldn't keep both identities from him.

"My daughter is quite a fan of yours, Miss Ross. She made me bring her down here from Charleston so she could hear your concert last night."

"Oh, were you at the concert?" Her heart pounded. She thought that he might hear her sing someday, though she always figured that she'd know when he was in the audience. If he had been there, he would surely have recognized the folk songs, for she sang those just as she had when she was a teenager.

"No, unfortunately, I didn't attend. I had several business deals to handle, but my daughter was very disappointed that she didn't get to meet you personally. Would you be kind enough to give me your autograph? It would make her day."

Genna reached into the backseat of the car for a large poster advertising her concert. She slashed Genna Ross in large letters across the bottom of it. Handing it to him, she said, "There, that should make her happy."

As she pulled away from the curb, she couldn't resist a peek through the rearview window. Evan stood on the sidewalk gazing after her.

three

Delivery trucks crowded the streets of Logan at the early hour when Genna, dressed in blue sweats, slipped out of her motel room. She wiped dew from the windows of the Mercedes and drove northward a few miles through the fog to Chief Logan State Park. Stepping out of the car she sniffed the air delightedly.

Too many years in the cities, she mused. *Why did I wait so long to come home*?

Other joggers and walkers greeted her with a wave and a frequent, "Good morning!" This was Appalachia, this was home. She hadn't jogged alone in years. Although often irritated by Jim's watchdog mentality, she'd had to admit that it wasn't wise for her to run alone in the cities where they usually stayed. But for now it was good to be alone, if only just to think. During this early morning run, however, she simply concentrated on the little brook meandering through the park, the maples and poplars along the pathway, and the chatter of songbirds.

The hour she spent among God's creation seemed to awaken Genna to her spiritual needs. She remembered some words Miss Amelia used to quote: "Exalt ye the Lord our God, and worship at his footstool; for he is holy." In the last few years

Genna had neglected her relationship to God. Now in the country, could she find the closeness to Him she'd once known? With Miss Amelia's help, she could. She'd be sure to visit the missionary.

The carefree run, and a brisk shower when she returned to the motel, gave Genna a vigor she hadn't known for months. Without Cary to style her hair, Genna blew it dry and let it hang loosely around her shoulders. She pushed aside most of her makeup and brushed a bit of gloss on her lips. Except for the change in hair color, she didn't look so different from Veevie Wooten. If she walked the streets of Logan looking like this, there were sure to be people who would recognize her.

Once she stepped out of this room as Veevie Wooten, it wouldn't be long before someone would also identify her as Genna Ross. The background she'd shielded so long would become common knowledge. If Evan had recognized her yesterday when he hadn't even attended her concert, many country music fans would be bound to put the two identities together.

But she'd come too far to go back now. She went to the cafe beside the motel and ordered a full breakfast. She felt as though she'd need the bacon, eggs, and hash browns to make it through the day. Coming home wasn't as pleasant as she'd anticipated.

She covered the miles from Logan to Mill Creek in less than an hour. *Guess my modern car goes a lot faster than Ben Fisher's truck*, she thought.

When she turned off the main highway to take

the Mill Creek road, Genna slowed down, partly because of the rough road but also because she wanted to see everything. The Sullivan No. 2 mine was still operating, obviously the interest that kept Evan in the area. Along the seven miles between the mine and the Fisher house, Genna counted only twelve residences that seemed to be occupied. Sadly she shook her head, remembering the many neighbors they'd had when she was a child.

Ivy and Ben lived in the same spot, but she was delighted to see a new mobile home instead of the rickety house they'd had in the past. She had paid them well for taking care of her place, so perhaps she'd contributed to their improved status. Not much else had changed though, she decided, when a beagle bounded off the porch to greet her. Ben wouldn't do without his dogs.

Ivy ran out and hugged her. "Law, Veevie, but you've changed. And what's happened to your hair?"

"Now, Ivy, it costs me a lot of money to have hair this color. Don't tell me you don't like it!"

Ben joined his wife and shook Genna's hand. "It's purty," he said. "Reminds me of that singer, Genna Ross."

Even though Ben must be in his early sixties, he was a stalwart man with a winning personality. A man of unhurried calm, he'd always displayed a sense of humor.

Genna threw her arms around him. "Oh, Ben, you remind me so much of Grandpap."

"Come on in, Veevie," Ivy invited.

"Say, I like your new home. You people are more prosperous than you used to be."

"After Ben lost his job in the mine, we had some hard times, but he took up carpentry and he's made a good livin' at that."

"Tell me the news," Genna invited. "What's going on around here?"

"I suppose you noticed the empty houses as you came up the creek."

"Yes. How long has Sullivan No. 1 been closed?"

"About five years. There ain't as much demand for coal as there once was. Our governor and senators are always tryin' to find new markets, and they've found some, but not enough to save the Sullivan mines. All of them have closed down except Sullivan No. 2 at the bottom of the hollow."

Genna's pulse quickened. "Then I don't suppose you see much of the Sullivans in Logan County."

"Evan Sullivan is around once in a while, seein' as he's still got some business interests here. That boy has had all kind of bad luck. I feel kinda sorry for him. He was always a good sort," Ben said.

"What's happened to him?" Genna asked, trying to sound casual in her questioning, but Ivy cast a speculative glance in her direction.

"First of all, his father died and left the business to him just about the time the mines began to close. Then, two or three years ago, his wife was killed in a car wreck that left him with a kid to raise," Ben said.

Genna's hands tightened on the arms of the

chair. She wanted to hear more, but emotion choked her and she changed the subject.

"What about the old homeplace? Do you think it's good enough for me to spend a few days there?"

"Hit ain't no mansion, Veevie. Never was, you know, but if you want to batch a little, no reason you couldn't," Ben said. "Still just got three rooms."

"You'd best eat with us, though," Ivy invited. "You're nuthin' but skin and bones."

"Unfortunately, I weigh more than I used to."

After lunch, Genna said, "I'll go up to the cabin now, if you'll let me have the key."

"You'd better not take that fancy car up there," Ben said. "Since nobody lives beyond here, the road ain't maintained. You can borrow my truck."

"My car isn't as fragile as you think. I'll drive slowly." She felt suddenly reluctant to visit her old home, and she went first to the family cemetery in the hollow behind the house. Ben had kept the small plot mowed, so Genna had no trouble finding Grandpap's grave, or that of her mother.

She stepped up on the front porch at last, and her hand trembled as she fitted the key into the lock. She'd had the lock installed before she left for California; the door had never been locked in Grandpap's day. Nothing had changed inside the house, except for its emptiness. Genna sat in Grandpap's old chair and the tears flowed, taking with them much of the bitterness she'd harbored.

Going to the car, she put on her jogging shoes.

Stuffing a package of cheese crackers and a can of cola in a sack, she headed toward Pinnacle Rock. Beset by greedy briers and fallen logs, she had a hard time keeping on the path. Loose rocks rolled under her feet, causing her to stumble. No one had traveled that way for a long time. Panting from exertion, she eventually came to the huge boulder. Even here changes greeted her. The oak tree had finally succeeded in cracking the rock and a large portion of it had tumbled down the mountainside. The rest of the rock looked as if it would endure forever.

She gasped audibly when she looked at the mountains across the creek. Brown and barren, strip miners had denuded the mountaintops of their crowning foliage. Of all the changes in her life, this one seemed the hardest to take. She had dreamed about this spot all of the years she'd been away, believing that despite the world's mercurial nature, Pinnacle Mountain and its surroundings would remain the same.

She lay back against the rock and sobbed as the past pulled at her heartstrings.

What had the Psalmist said? "I lift up my eyes to the hills—where does my help come from? My help comes from the Lord, the Maker of heaven and earth."

As much as she loved the hills, she knew that they were temporal things and no strength could be gained from them. She'd long known that only God could supply her needs, but she'd allowed herself to lose contact with Him.

A sound behind her startled Genna out of her reverie and she turned quickly, swiping at her eyes.

Evan Sullivan looked at her reproachfully. "So it was you. Why did you lie to me?"

"I don't remember our conversation exactly, but I don't believe I lied. I am Genna Ross now."

She turned away from him, overcome by sadness and yearning. She still longed for him, and having learned this morning that he no longer had a wife made a difference. But she mustn't forget how he'd wronged her years ago.

Without an invitation, Evan climbed to sit beside her on the rock. "You've come a long way, Veevie, from the last time I saw you here. I'd like to hear about it."

"Grandpap knew that he wouldn't live very long after he contracted black lung, and he made provisions for me. He made me promise lots of things before he died, and one of them was that I'd go to live with my Cousin Bea in California. Grandpap never spent much money, and when the mines were going strong he'd made good wages. He put his savings in a trust fund for me. I didn't want to leave the mountains, but I was alone and didn't have much choice."

"It was several months before I heard your grandfather had died. I would have helped you if I'd known."

Genna stared at him with hostile green eyes, and Evan's face flushed.

"When I got to California, even though I'd

graduated from high school, Cousin Bea hired a tutor for a year to take off my rough edges. You'll remember, I had lots of them; you'd pointed that out to me."

Genna ignored the plea in Evan's eyes and continued, her voice growing more harsh the longer she spoke.

"She knew that I'd never make it through college without learning better grammar and some basic subjects I'd not had. I went through four years of college, and right from the first, I excelled in drama. I starred in several college productions, and in my senior year, a talent scout spotted me and thought I had the capability to achieve success as a singer. He was right, and in about six months, Genna Ross was born. My advisors considered 'Veevie Wooten' a handicap, so I adopted a stage name. Genna is a derivative of Genevieve as Veevie had been."

"I'm not a country music fan, so I haven't followed your career, but what puzzles me is why no one in Logan County guessed who you are."

Genna shrugged her shoulders. "I've not kept in touch with anyone here except Ben and Ivy, and I've never told them about my career. Cousin Bea died the year I graduated from college, so her family didn't know what I was doing. A lawyer in Logan has handled my trust account, and I contact him periodically. In all my local business transactions I use the name Genevieve Wooten."

"Looks like you covered your tracks very well," Evan observed.

Genna nodded and set the crackers and drink on the rock. "Want to share my snack?"

"Kinda like old times, don't you think?" He smiled, but Genna ignored his comment.

"I've been surprised myself," she continued. "It would be like some magazine writer to uproot my past, but I haven't given them any leads. By the time I'd started my career, I'd lost my mountain talk. A few good drama teachers had taken away my Appalachian colloquialisms, so I couldn't be traced to the hills that way."

"Then why come back now? If you stay around here, your past will be revealed."

"When I received the invitation to perform that benefit show, I remembered how Grandpap had suffered from black lung. I decided to come back for that, and the nearer the time came, the more I longed to be home again. Afterward I sent my crew back to Nashville. I wanted to be alone."

"But what if you're recognized? Are you ashamed of what you used to be?"

She turned on him angrily. "I was never ashamed of what I was. I've never been ashamed of Grandpap. It was the dread of seeing you, Evan, that prevented me from returning, kept me from revealing my roots. But now that I've been unfortunate enough to encounter you, I'm going to burn all of my bridges behind me. I'm ready to reveal my dual life. My fans won't hold it against me that I'm a moonshiner's granddaughter, that I used to say 'hit,' 'ain't,' and 'you-all.'"

"That's a strike below the belt, Veevie. I suppose

you still haven't forgiven me?"

"I suppose I haven't. Would you expect me to?"

She stood up. "Time to get off of this mountain before nightfall. As you probably discovered, the trail isn't in good shape. Nobody else has wanted to use it, I guess."

"I came up here for several years, hoping you'd come back, but I finally gave up."

Without answering, she started down the mountain with Evan following silently behind her. His truck was parked beside her Mercedes at the cabin.

"Veevie, I wish you'd give me a chance to explain. I wanted to ten years ago when you ran away. I tried for months to trace you, asked everyone in Logan County I could think of."

"You must not have asked the right persons. A few people knew where I was, but it was too late to explain then anyway."

"Will you listen to my explanation now?"

"Come in, if you want to. Sorry I can't offer you any food. I brought only a few things with me and I won't be here long. Let's sit on the porch."

They sat silently for several minutes. The sun's orb hovered over the mountain peak and long shadows fell across the yard. Genna heard a fish flip-flop in Mill Creek. A robin hopped pertly through the grass, only to stop abruptly before pulling a struggling worm from the ground.

Genna wished that her heart would stop racing as she gazed intently on her stage-perfect manicure. She couldn't look at Evan. *Why couldn't she overcome the attraction this man held for her*? But

Genna was an actress, and she willed her hands to relax on the chair arms as she rocked serenely in Grandpap's old rocker.

"Do you know that my wife is no longer living?"

"Cousin Ivy mentioned that this morning. Otherwise, I'd not have listened to you at all."

"When I left you on your sixteenth birthday, I had no idea but to come back to see you, but all kinds of things happened. I went away to school and didn't come home very often."

"Had your father learned about me, and that's the reason he kept you away?"

"Probably. But the longer I went without seeing you, I began to forget, and I started dating Marsha. She was the kind of woman Dad thought I should marry, and before I knew it, I was engaged to her. By that time, Dad wanted me in the business with him, and we married and moved to Charleston."

"So you patterned your life the way your father wanted it?"

"I suppose so. Gradually, my memories of you faded into the background. My marriage wasn't happy, but I blamed no one but myself. Marsha hated the hills. The only happy part of that marriage is my child, Michelle. I didn't love my wife, but I love my daughter."

"Is that your explanation then? All you have to say for yourself?"

"There isn't much else I can say except to ask your forgiveness. The need to do that has haunted me for years."

"Forgive you? Yes, I suppose I do. I forgive you for

marrying someone else. You had a perfect right to do that, but I do think you could have told me and not left me to find out in a most embarrassing manner. The least you could have done was to have told me."

Genna tried to control her voice, but in spite of herself, all of the bitterness came rushing out unharnessed.

"I was ashamed to write to you, Veevie. I thought that you must have found out some other way. You didn't write to me or make any move to keep in touch. I wrote you one letter after I went to California, but you didn't answer it."

"No, because I didn't want to annoy you with my lack of education. I spent two years trying to make myself suitable for you. Grandpap used his precious money to straighten my teeth. I studied hard, had Miss Amelia, the missionary, help me with my grammar, tried so hard to be the kind of person you wanted. Even after a silence of two years, I hoped you hadn't changed, that you still wanted me. Then I came to your office to be confronted with the truth."

Evan left his chair and wandered to the edge of the porch, putting his arm around one of the posts. His other hand nervously jingled the change in his pocket.

"Put that way, the bald truth sounds pretty bad, and I don't blame you for feeling bitter, Veevie. I've never blamed you. Right from the first, I've placed all the blame on myself, but that doesn't make my guilt any easier to live with."

Genna rose slowly, finding she had to lean

against the rocker for support.

"Evan, I thank you for the explanation. You've done what you wanted to do and I really think that's all we have to say to each other. I don't have any desire to resurrect the past. In a few days I'll be leaving here, and I don't know when, if ever, I'll return. I have a busy winter concert schedule."

He turned toward her and, thinking she might never see him again, Genna looked intently at the close-cropped beard and the gray eyes that seemed hooded with grief. His youthful face had haunted her for years; this time, she'd have the picture of a mature Evan to carry with her.

"You may not have anything more to say to me, my dear, but I haven't finished. The love I had for you when you were a girl has never changed. It was only after you were gone that I realized how much I cherished you, how much I'd lost. Ten years of loneliness hasn't cured me of that. I'm not sure anything will ever change the way I feel about you. Goodnight, Veevie."

Genna sat on the top step of the cabin porch for a long time after Evan left. The sound of katydids droned in her ears and lightning bugs flitted through the darkness. Dry-eyed, she finally trudged into the house and prepared for bed, but she lay until morning without any thought of sleep. Evan wasn't the only one who realized how much had been lost.

four

"Okay, Cary. I'm awake," Genna mumbled, but the pounding on the door continued. She blinked her eyes a few times and realized that she had awakened at the old homestead.

Struggling out of the feather bed, she threw a robe over her gown and rushed to the door. A burly man wearing a hard hat was poised on the edge of the porch. He turned, bug-eyed, when Genna appeared.

Genna's eyes swept the yard crowded with two dump trucks, an end-loader, and a bulldozer. Several men stood beside her car peering at the interior. She stared at a sign nailed to a porch post.

CONDEMNED. NO TRESPASSING, STAY OUT!

"What do you mean by putting that sign on my house?" she shouted. Reminding herself of Grandpap, she tore the cardboard off the post and threw it on the ground.

"Ma'am, we were told this house was vacant, but I wondered what that Mercedes was doing out here in the yard."

"Don't evade the question. Why did you nail up that sign? What's all this machinery doing on my property?"

"I'm a foreman for the Keystone Mining Company. We're starting to mine in this hollow. This house is in the way of our operations and we have to destroy it to make a road for our mining equipment."

"Over my dead body, you'll strip that hollow." She ran back into the house and returned with Grandpap's shotgun. "Or over your dead body! This property will never be strip-mined. Move that equipment out of here immediately!"

"Now, ma'am, listen to reason."

Genna lifted the gun and fired into the air above the man's head.

Good old Grandpap! He always kept a shell in this gun. Genna rubbed her arm where the gun had kicked her. *I'll sure get chewed out by Cary if that leaves a bruise*, she thought.

The workers scattered like quail and the foreman jumped inside a pickup. "I'm going to get the sheriff. You ain't got no reason to shoot at me. This property was sold for back taxes."

Genna darted into the house, threw on a sweatshirt and a pair of jeans and picked up her purse, then ran across the yard to the Mercedes. As she dashed away, she called out the window. "I'm going to call the sheriff myself. Don't touch one thing on this property or you'll live to regret it."

At a speed too fast for the unimproved road, she rushed the mile to Ivy's house. Ben must have seen her coming and he met her on the porch.

"What's up, Veevie?"

"There's a group of miners up at the house saying they've bought the property and are going to start stripping there. I want to call my lawyer. Let me use your phone."

"He won't be in his office this early."

"I'll call him at home then. I promised Grandpap that I'd never let his property be strip-mined." Her fingers trembled until she had trouble dialing the numbers.

"Mr. Blankenship," she said when a sleepy voice answered the phone. "This is Genevieve Wooten, and I'm in trouble." Breathlessly, she explained about her early morning visitors.

"That's impossible, Miss Wooten. I've paid those taxes faithfully from your trust fund, just as you instructed me."

"Then will you take steps immediately to stop them? Bring the sheriff out here and halt these workers until we can find out the mistake. Grandpap will turn over in his grave if they lift one shovel of dirt."

"I'll be out in an hour. Can you keep them from starting until then?"

"Yes. I've already peppered one of them with a shotgun blast. I figure there's some more shells around someplace."

"Veevie," Ben said when she hung up the phone, "you don't mean you shot at them fellers. That old gun of your grandpap's always hits the mark." Ivy pushed a cup of coffee into Genna's hand.

"I shot over his head." She sipped a little of the coffee and handed the cup back to Ivy. "Come with me, Ben. I may need some help until Mr. Blankenship arrives. I took them by surprise, but if they use force, there isn't much I can do against five men."

"Yeah, I'll go. Wait'll I get my gun."

Genna looked in the mirror over the couch. Her disheveled blond hair scattered over her shoulders and her sleepy eyes looked small without makeup. No one could possibly mistake her for Genna Ross the way she looked now, she thought wryly.

Ben climbed into the passenger seat of the Mercedes and held on to the dashboard when Genna lurched out of his yard.

"Do you always drive this fast, Veevie?"

The goldenrod blooming along the road turned into a blurred yellow streak as she floored the accelerator.

"Only when I'm in a hurry. Lance would have a fit if he saw me treating the car this way, but he didn't pay for it."

"Who's Lance? Did you get married while you've been away?"

"No, I'm not married. Lance is my chauffeur."

Ben whistled. "You got a chauffeur? You've gone up in the world since we've seen you."

"I've gone up far enough that I don't intend to let some thief steal my property."

The five men were huddled together in front of a dump truck when Genna rounded the bend. By the time she stopped her car, they were in the vehicles with the windows closed. Genna pecked on the window of the foreman's pickup. He lowered the window a crack.

"My lawyer and the sheriff are on their way out here. Don't you make a move until then," Genna cautioned him.

Ben settled himself on the porch step, his rifle over his knees. "Go freshen up, Veevie. I'll stop the critters if they try any funny stuff."

Genna hurried inside and twisted her billowing hair into a barrette. Noting from the window that Ben still had things under control, she sat at the kitchen table in an attempt to still her trembling knees.

A sweet roll and a container of orange juice wasn't much of a breakfast, but it did soothe her spirit. When she went back to the porch, she picked up Grandpap's gun and joined Ben on the steps.

They stayed seated when a sheriff's car drove in behind the mining equipment. George Blankenship stepped from the car with a deputy sheriff behind him and together they approached the house.

"You two are looking warlike."

The Keystone foreman ventured out of the truck. "That woman shot at me. I want her arrested."

"You can't have a woman arrested for protecting her property," Blankenship said, looking sternly at the man. "Where's your deed for this property?"

"I can't carry a deed around in my pocket. The Keystone Mining Company has bought up the land on the east side of the mountain, and I was sent to start work. Here are my orders and the survey of the land."

After flipping through the papers the foreman handed him, Blankenship said, "This property is included in your orders all right, but somebody has made a mistake. I've paid the taxes on this place for ten years and I have the receipts to prove it but they're in the bank vault. I can't get in there on Saturday, and the courthouse is closed too. I did contact the county judge, however, and he issued a temporary restraining order to stop this work for a week until we get the matter straightened out."

The Keystone employee appealed to the deputy. "Does that mean we can't work today?"

The deputy nodded. "Not today, not for a week."

"Can we leave this machinery here until then?"

"No," Genna said. "I came home for a visit to enjoy myself. I can't do it if I see that machinery. Move it now."

The man swore under his breath and turned on his heel. After a conference with his men, he motioned them to follow him and they rattled noisily down the road.

"Thanks, Mr. Blankenship. I'm sorry to bother you, but you know what Grandpap thought of strip miners. I sure am glad that I happened to be home. What next?"

"I'll arrange a meeting with the management of the Keystone Mining Company to prove we're in our rights. These men," he motioned to the departing workers, "can't make any decisions. They're only following orders. Will you be around a few days?"

"Yes, at least until we get this straightened out."

"I'll set the appointment as early in the week as possible."

"Leave word with Ben; I'll check there."

Watching Blankenship and the deputy leaving, Ben laid his gun aside. "Well, you won that round."

Genna didn't answer, but she felt Ben's keen glance on her. He smiled slightly. "Veevie, I've been puttin' two and two together, and though Ivy says I'm crazy, I've come up with an answer. How far wrong would I be if I added Veevie Wooten and your sudden appearance back in Logan County, and came up with the answer, Genna Ross?"

Genna stretched her long legs and looked out over the hollow, peaceful once more now that the mining equipment was gone.

"I'd have to give you an A plus, Ben."

"Just what I figgered. Ivy and me went to that benefit show over in Woodville three nights ago. All the time you was performin,' I thought you seemed familiar, 'specially when you sung them mountain songs. 'Course I'd seen you on television a few times and then your picture is always on your records. I knew hit was far-fetched, but when you showed up here a couple days after the concert, I thought hit had to be you. Why haven't you told us? People in Logan County would have been mighty proud to know one of our own had gone to the top. How come you changed your name?"

Genna shrugged her shoulders. "Many singers take stage names, and I liked the sound of Genna Ross. I've always kept my real name on legal papers, and I use it when I correspond with Blankenship. He knows my professional name, but

I suppose he guarded that as an attorney-client confidence."

"We won't say anything if you don't want hit known. I thought maybe you was kinda ashamed of your kin here at home."

"No, that isn't true. I don't intend to hide my past any longer. Reporters love this kind of story. Once they learn about my rags to riches background, they'll spread it everywhere and I'll get lots of free publicity. I knew when I came back here my roots would probably be revealed, but Ben, I was homesick."

He patted her on the shoulder. "Becomin' rich and famous hasn't made you happy then?"

Tears glistened in her eyes, and she wiped them away angrily. "No, it hasn't. Someplace along the way I've lost more than I've gained. I don't know that I'm searching for happiness, but I would like to know serenity and peace of mind again. I believe I could find it here."

"Why don't you stay with us a while? These old hills have helped more than one person get a right outlook on life."

"Ben, I can't stay long this time. I've a full schedule for the next six months. My business manager had a fit when I told him I was taking this two-week vacation. Last night when I couldn't sleep I made some decisions. I'm coming back home."

"Good for you, Veevie, or should I call you Genna now?"

"I don't much care. Last night I had a longing to

be here in the springtime—to watch the serviceberry trees herald the coming of spring, to walk in the woods and see the blooming dogwood, the redbud blossoms, to listen to the whipporwills."

"Hit's a good time to be in this hollow."

"I'm booked through next March, but I'll tell Jim not to schedule anything for the spring months. The first of April, I'm coming home for an extended stay." She patted the post beside her. "Do you think we could make this old cabin more livable—add a bathroom, put in central heat, and the like?"

Ben walked around the house with her and helped her make plans. "I wouldn't want to change the structure of the house, but I could insulate it and put vinyl siding on the exterior, and maybe panel the three downstairs rooms. There's pretty kitchen paneling available now, as well as woodgrains for the other two rooms. We could put in electric baseboard heat too."

"Yes, but I'd still want to retain the old fireplace. I spent some cozy times in front of it with Grandpap." *And Evan, too,* her conscience tormented her.

"Here in the back, you could build a new room for a bath without changing the looks of the place."

They wandered back to the spring house and Genna stuck her head into the damp interior. She filled a tin cup full of the cold liquid that had dribbled into a tank imbedded in the dirt floor.

"Don't suppose I'd have any trouble with the

water supply?"

"Nope, that water has been seepin' out of Pinnacle Mountain since I first remember. Hit'll always be there."

"If the Keystone Company doesn't ruin it when they start stripping the east side of the mountain," Genna added bitterly.

"Might happen," Ben agreed, "but let's hope not. You could put a little pump here in the spring house, and with a few feet of pipe laid underground you'd be in good shape."

"I'd keep most of the old furniture, but I'm going to discard that feather tick for a waterbed. It will take fifteen minutes every morning to get the kinks out of my back after a night spent in that bed."

Ben laughed. "Years ago when we didn't know any better, we thought a feather bed was a luxury. I slept on a cornhusk mattress when I was a youngun. You keep wantin' to revive the past, Veevie, but all of it wasn't good."

"I'm finding that out the more I remember."

"Want us to do this remodelin' for you next winter while you're gone—have it all ready when you come in the spring?"

"No, I think not. I want the fun of doing it myself."

"I'd better head back down to the house or Ivy will think we've been hauled off to jail."

"I'll drive you, but I don't want to be away from here too long—I still don't trust the Keystone Company."

"I think that restrainin' order will hold them off all right, but I can see your point. If you're gone, I'll keep an eye open. They won't bring that equipment up this creek without me seein' them."

"Ben, I've been wanting to ask, is the missionary Miss Amelia still around here? I don't want to leave without seeing her."

"Yeah, she's still rattlin' around these hollers in her old VW visitin' saints and sinners alike. You'll find her in the same place."

After leaving Ben at home Genna drove on down the hollow to Miss Amelia's small cottage.

Of all the former places and people Genna had seen so far, Amelia Dixon had changed the least. Short and lean as ever but still spry, Miss Amelia was blessed with the keenest blue eyes Genna had ever seen. Amelia said warmly, "Veevie! I thought you'd never come to see us again. Come in."

The living room was cluttered with the many items Miss Amelia had accumulated through the years. Genna walked around the room, touched the keys of the upright piano, and moved her hands along the replica of the praying hands on the mantle. On the end table beside Miss Amelia's recliner the familiar, well-worn King James Bible had been replaced by a modern translation—the only evidence of the passage of time.

Perhaps sensing that Genna was having trouble controlling her emotions, Amelia allowed her to browse in silence.

With a wistful smile, Genna sat on the stool beside Amelia's chair. "So at last I've found something that's unchangeable. Miss Amelia, I feel as if I've come home at last."

"When you've changed so much, you have no right to expect everything else to remain static. You've been gone a long time. Are you home to stay, Veevie?"

Genna shook her head and, at Amelia's invitation, launched into a full description of her life in California and her rise to fame. She paused only when Amelia handed her a cup of hot tea.

But Amelia, like Ben, had read the hidden meaning of Genna's story. "So you've acquired everything but happiness?"

With eyes downcast, Genna nodded. "Can you give me words from that to fill the void I have?" She motioned to the Bible. "You always used to do that. More than once I've come here disheartened and you said the magic words that perked me up again."

Miss Amelia's hand moved toward the Bible, but first she lifted Genna's head, forcing her to look into her eyes. Genna flushed, happy that she had nothing to hide from that piercing gaze.

"So you've stayed decent then? I had to know."

"Yes," Genna said simply.

"Forgive me for being rude, but out in the world where you were, it must have been quite a struggle to live morally pure."

Genna shook her head. "On the contrary. Not once during the building of my career have I ever felt any temptation to do otherwise. I've had many offers, but the temptation wasn't there."

Genna had phrased those words carefully. They were true during the building of her career, but Evan had tempted her. She had never forgotten her feelings for him and no one since Evan had rekindled them.

"So much for your morality—what about your spiritual life?"

Miss Amelia had always been one to drive right to the heart of a matter; Genna complied with a direct answer. "I haven't been to church since Bea died, Miss Amelia. When we're out on tour, usually we travel all day on Sunday. Weekends are the busiest time for us. I'm not using that as an excuse. It was just easy to stop going."

"Yet you're looking for that which is unchanged, when the greatest change in you is the neglect of your faith." Genna nodded. "And I seem to remember that someplace in the Bible, it says, 'I am the Lord, I change not.' "

"Yes, that's in Malachi. Seems to me, Veevie, that all you've achieved has been a gift from God, and I feel He must be disappointed in how you've neglected Him. If you don't have time for spiritual growth, you're too busy."

Genna nodded. "I know. I need one of your down-to-earth sermons. I think that's one reason I had to revisit the hills. It's as though I'd lost something that I can only regain here, but I can see now that I won't find it right away. I took a long time going away from the Lord; I have to work my way back. Will you pray for me?"

"I always do, Genna." She smiled as she took

Genna's hand. "It's going to be hard to remember the new name."

"Doesn't matter. It's rather nice to hear Veevie again."

"Let's pray now before you go." Genna knelt beside the chair and felt the missionary's hands on her hair. The years retracted and she was a teenager again, hurt by Evan's rejection, suffering from insults by her peers, longing for a day of reckoning. That day had come now, she supposed, but somehow it wasn't as sweet as she had thought it might be.

While she still knelt, Miss Amelia said, "You wanted a Bible verse: 'Do not conform any longer to the pattern of this world, but be transformed by the renewing of your mind. Then you will be able to test and approve what God's will is—his good, pleasing and perfect will.' "

Genna's eyes misted when she stood up.

"Go to church with me tomorrow," Miss Amelia invited.

Genna hesitated a bit. *Was she ready for that*? But she agreed. "Where will we go?"

"To Bethel, of course. You'll see a few people you know, but there are some changes too."

A brick church, complete with factory-built pews, had replaced the small wooden structure with its rustic hand-hewn benches. A carpeted area housed a pulpit and a communion table. The old upright piano had been abandoned for a spinet. Nothing seemed familiar to Genna as she prepared her heart for the pastor's message. His text from

Isaiah 58:12, however, proved significant: "Your people will rebuild the ancient ruins and will raise up the age-old foundations."

Her foundations hadn't been destroyed, but she needed to rebuild her spiritual values. While the pastor talked, she tried to reason out those foundations that had once sustained her spiritually.

Ben hailed her when she approached the Fisher home after leaving the church. She pulled over and he stuck his head into the car window. "Ivy's got a picnic lunch packed. Go home and change your clothes and we'll come for you in the truck."

Genna hurried into her jeans and sweatshirt and waited on the porch when Ben drove into the yard. When Ivy scooted over and made room for Genna, Genna said, "No, I want to ride in the back. It will be more like old times."

She stepped on the bumper and jumped into the pickup bed, dodged a weed trimmer, picnic basket, and thermos jug, and leaned back against the truck's cab.

"Hold on," Ben called. "We're goin' to the head of the holler, and hit's a rough road."

A haze hung over the area, a sure sign of Indian summer, and a flock of bluejays began squawking their displeasure at this human invasion of their sanctuary. Not many vehicles traveled this old road anymore, Genna surmised, although it had been a busy area when the coal mine at the head of the hollow had operated.

That had been the mine where Grandpap had last worked, but it closed about the time he'd had to retire. A few more years and there would be nothing left of the thriving coal operation of twenty years ago.

Ben gunned the engine and the pickup climbed steadily along the side of Pinnacle Mountain. Genna strained her eyes to see the rock outcropping where she and Evan had met on Friday but they were too close to the base of the mountain. Ben stopped the truck near the edge of the lake. Even here decay had set in. The picnic tables were barely visible in a field of blooming sunflowers, wingstems, and goldenrod.

"Doesn't anyone use this anymore?"

"There's no one around to use it. Very few young people live on Mill Creek now and them that do have cars. Hit's more fun to go to Logan or to stay home and watch videos than to come skatin' or swimmin' at this old dam," Ivy said.

Ben took the weed trimmer from the truck. "I'll cut the weeds away from one of the tables. We don't want a rattler picnickin' with us, or if he does, I want to see him first."

"We knew the place had run down, but we thought you might enjoy a picnic like we used to have."

"We did have some good times, Ivy, and I want you to know I appreciate how good you were to Grandpap and me. You helped us pass many a lonely Sunday by bringing us here on picnics."

Genna walked around the lake on a deer trail while Ivy and Ben prepared the lunch table. Run-off water from the mountain had collected through the years behind an impoundment that the mine company had built out of refuse from the mine. At this point Mill Creek was formed by two mountain streams, and the mining company had dammed the left-hand fork by dumping slag from the mine. For every load of coal they removed from underground, the miners also brought out slag—a mixture of shale, clay, and mine dust.

The miners needed a place to dispose of this refuse, and since a supply of water was required to clean the coal, the impoundment served two purposes—disposal for the slag, and from that, collection of the water they needed.

Genna paused on the crest of the fifteen-foot-high impoundment. While the mine operated, the water had been too dirty for any recreational purpose; once the mine had closed, however, the impurities had settled to the bottom. Although the coal company, which still owned the site, had put up NO TRESPASSING signs, local residents had eventually built picnic tables on the sides of the lake. Most residents were afraid to swim in the water, but in winter, skaters had often built bonfires on the banks and spent many a cold evening sliding over the frozen lake.

Ben joined Genna. "I wish they'd destroy this thing—let the water out gradually. I've been afeared of it ever since that Buffalo Creek disaster a few years ago."

Genna remembered distinctly that February day in 1972. A forty-five-foot-high impoundment had broken at the head of Buffalo Creek spilling a twenty-acre lake down the valley. Several towns had been destroyed with a loss of 125 lives. Ben, who'd helped with the rescue efforts, had never forgotten those shattering days, and the memories caused him to be wary of the hundreds of other such impoundments scattered throughout mining country.

Genna glanced at the water behind them. "There's not as much water here as in the impoundments on Buffalo Creek."

"No, but the conditions are the same. This dam rests on a spongy base of silt and sludge, and though the water looks clear enough now, there's all kinds of junk on the bottom of that lake—metal and wooden refuse from the mines. In winter, when we've had lots of rain, this whole dam is squishy."

"Who's responsible for maintaining it?"

"The mine company still owns the land, but hit's hard to get them to do anything. We've approached the state and federal agencies, but hit's one of those situations where people pass the buck. I am goin' to call someone about that soft spot over there." He motioned toward their right, where oozing water had soaked one portion of the dam.

Genna locked her arm through his. "It won't collapse today," she said brightly, "so let's enjoy our picnic."

"That's what everybody says—just keep puttin' hit off another day. One of these days hit'll be too late," Ben grumbled. His face etched in worry, he good-naturedly let Genna propel him toward the picnic table where he helped himself to Ivy's spread of fried chicken, baked beans, and potato salad.

five

The next morning, still wallowing in nostalgia, Genna climbed the narrow steps to the loft room that had been her bedroom when she was a girl. She removed the curtain from the one small window and lighted the oil lamp on the dresser. Ivy must clean the room often, she thought, as the feather tick on the twin bed was neatly fashioned and not a speck of dust or dirt was evident.

Genna pulled the curtain away from the closet. The clothes she'd left behind when she went to California still hung there. She lifted the white dress she'd bought to wear to the senior prom, hoping Evan would come back and serve as her escort. She'd never worn the dress. She smiled wryly as she compared these garments with the designer clothes she now wore.

In a dresser drawer Genna found some pictures she'd cherished years ago. The top photo of a smiling brunette elicited a delighted response. "Angela Minton! I haven't thought of her for years."

Angela had been Veevie's only close friend. Her father had worked at the Miller mine and then had moved on to work for the Sullivans when they started mining operations in the county. Angela had been Veevie's confidante, and the only person to whom she'd revealed her love for Evan. Because Angela's father had once been in prison, she was outside the pale of society, too, so the two girls had comforted one another. They'd corresponded for a year or so after she left, but she hadn't had any contact with her friend for a long time.

When Genna went to the Fishers' for lunch, she asked, "What ever happened to Angela Minton? I found a picture of her today and it sure brought back memories."

"It should have," Ben said. "A feller would be hard put to find two more giggly girls."

"She lives in Woodville," Ivy answered, ignoring Ben's comment. "She's Angela Keefer now."

"Maybe I'll go and see her this afternoon."

"She works someplace, so you'd better wait until after supper."

Genna contemplated a visit with her friend most of the afternoon. Following Ben's directions, she drove into Woodville about four o'clock and found Angela's residence. The one-story frame house was freshly painted white and green shutters framed the windows. The grass had been cut recently and flowers were attractively grouped around the yard.

Angela wasn't home yet so Genna rolled down the window of the car and waited. She'd been there about an hour when a blue Chevrolet pulled into the driveway. The woman who emerged looked inquiringly at the Mercedes parked in front of her house.

It's Angela all right, Genna laughed to herself, as she hurried from her car to Angela's side. "Do you remember me? I'm Veevie Wooten."

"You can't be," Angela said. "If you tell me you're Genna Ross, I'll believe that."

Genna could tell that Angela wasn't joking; she really didn't recognize her childhood friend.

"Don't you remember the time we stayed all night with Ben and Ivy, and after they went to sleep, we slipped out and went skinny-dipping in the creek?"

Angela laughed. "You must be Veevie! We didn't tell anyone else about that. Come on in."

"Are you too busy for us to talk over old times this evening? I could go buy a pizza for dinner."

"I have to leave around seven o'clock, but we can visit until then. While you go after the pizza, I'll change my clothes and make a salad. Iced tea sound good to you?"

"Yes, that's fine. Is your tea as good as what Ivy used to prepare when we went on picnics?"

"Probably not. I've learned that most foods don't taste as good as they did when we were children."

When Genna returned with the pizza, she said, "Angela, I must tell you the truth first. When you said I was Genna Ross, well, you were right."

Angela set down the pitcher of iced tea with a thud. "I didn't see how I could be mistaken. I saw your show last week, and I recognized you instantly when you got out of the car. I've thought of you so often, Veevie, and wondered what had happened to you."

She burst into laughter when she brought the rotary cutter to divide the pizza.

"What's so funny?"

"I suddenly remembered what they wrote about you in the class prophecy—that in ten years, you'd be working as a waitress in Bob's Bar and Grill."

"If I remember, you didn't receive a glowing prophecy for the future either."

"No, I was to marry a miner and have five children."

"Well, how far wrong is that prediction? What have you been up to since I've seen you?"

"After our graduation, I was at loose ends for a while. I wanted to go to business school but Dad was out of work and we had no money. But Miss Amelia, bless her heart, scurried around and secured some grants for me and I went to college, majoring in business administration and music."

"I remember that you always played the piano for our sing-alongs with Miss Amelia."

"She'd given me enough lessons that I had sufficient background to enroll in advanced music classes."

"What are you doing now?"

"I give private piano lessons and play the organ at the Methodist church. To make a living, I'm the business administrator at the hospital."

"No husband?"

"My husband died two years ago with cancer. We had no children. Now tell me everything about yourself."

Since it was apparent that Angela was interested in her career, Genna talked at length about her accomplishments.

Once Angela interrupted with a smile. "I don't hear anything about any romantic attachments — hasn't the great Genna Ross broken lots of hearts?"

Genna bit her lip and shook her head.

"You've never gotten over Evan, have you?" Angela said keenly. "The way you loved him was almost an obsession. I didn't think you'd ever forget him. By the way, have you seen Evan?"

"Yes, unfortunately! He's the reason I haven't come home before this. I thought I could avoid him this one time, but as luck would have it, I've seen him twice."

"Hey, I just thought of this—that's the reason you wrote 'One-man Woman.' "

"Yes, I had him in mind when I was writing. The same way with a new song to be released soon, 'Why Do I Love Him?' I hoped writing about him would make the past go away, but you can see it didn't work." Suddenly Genna glanced at her watch. "It's half past six, Angela. I've got to go or you'll be late for your appointment."

"Why don't you come with me? Miss Amelia and I are going to a little church up in Pickett Hollow for an evening service. The congregation doesn't have a preacher, so Miss Amelia goes up each Monday evening for Bible study. I go along to provide the music."

Genna glanced down at her jeans. "What about

my clothes?"

"Everybody dresses casually these days. I'm wearing slacks, too."

Miss Amelia arrived in her VW about fifteen minutes later, and she smiled when she saw Genna and Angela together.

"Just like old times. I meant to tell you Sunday that Angela still lived in the area. I'm going to expect a song out of you, Genna."

"I don't know what it would be. I never sing church songs."

"High time you did then," Miss Amelia said crisply. "You can find something in one of the hymnals."

Genna took the back seat and watched with interest as Miss Amelia drove north out of Woodville. After a couple of miles, she left the paved road and wound her way up a small creek valley. Fifteen minutes later, she stopped beside a white frame church perched on the side of a hill.

When they entered the building, Genna was taken back to the sanctuary of her childhood. The room was sparsely furnished with a few wooden benches and an old, battered pulpit. When Angela ran her hands across the stained keys of the old upright, Genna noted the piano was sadly in need of tuning.

The congregation was small, but what they lacked in numbers, they made up in enthusiasm. Genna joined them in their joyful singing of hymns she hadn't heard for years. "I Saw The Light," "When The Roll Is Called Up Yonder," and

"Sweet By and By" rolled off her tongue as easily as if she'd sung them yesterday.

Knowing that Miss Amelia intended for her to sing during the testimony meeting, Genna leafed through the pages of the tattered hymnal. When the missionary introduced her, Genna had decided on "Where Could I Go?"

She gave the words a Genna Ross flavor and the worshipers sat spellbound. She tried her best not to make it a performance but strictly a song of worship. On the way home Genna sat quietly remembering the words of the chorus. The Psalmist had lifted his eyes to the hills, but where could she turn for help? The song had given her the answer.

Where could I go, oh, where could I go
Seeking a refuge for my soul.
Needing a friend to save me in the end,
Where could I go but to the Lord?

When Miss Amelia stopped at Angela's house, she held Genna's hand for a minute. "Thanks for singing tonight. You have a great talent, but have you ever considered you might not be using it in the right way?"

No mistake this time—someone was pounding on the door.

"Veevie!" Ben's yell pierced her semiconscious state. "You awake?"

She threw on a robe and made an attempt to open the bedroom window. It squeaked from disuse, but she finally forced it up a few inches.

"Here I am, Ben. What do you want?"

He sauntered off the porch toward her. "Blankenship phoned. The hearin' with Keystone is at eleven o'clock. He said to meet him at his office. Had your breakfast yet?"

"No," Genna answered groggily.

"Ivy said for me to fetch you down to eat with us."

"One of her breakfasts sounds better than anything I have here. Wonder if she'd mind if I shower down there?"

"Nope. Come down when you want to."

She forced the window back into place and checked the few clothes she'd brought with her. The skirt and blouse she'd worn recently needed laundering. Wrinkling her nose, she murmured, "Nothing suitable for a judge's office. He'd probably cite me for contempt of court if I show up in sweats or jeans."

Mired in indecision, she finally put on the shirt and jeans she'd worn yesterday. Walking to the car, she shivered in the brisk air. The maple leaves in the yard showed a tinge of yellow in the morning sun. She had to halt the Mercedes at the road's edge to permit the passing of a low-bed truck hauling a bulldozer. At first she thought it was more Keystone Mining equipment heading her way, but the truck bounced on up the road and around the bend.

When Genna pulled up at Ben and Ivy's her concerns about the bulldozer were behind her.

Ben greeted her with an update. "I called the company about that leak in the sludge pond, and those fellers are aimin' to fix hit, I reckon."

Genna passed on into the kitchen. "Is there any place in Logan where I can buy dress clothes? I didn't plan to be here except a few days and I brought only casual things. Who'd believe I'd become involved in a lawsuit!"

Ivy placed grits and bacon on the table and returned to the stove for the biscuits. "There's some good stores in Logan along that second street back from the river. You recollect where it is?"

"Yes. I'll go early and try to find a suit. I need more clothes like I need a hole in my head, but I want to look respectable."

Ben drew up his chair and dropped his head for a quick blessing. Reaching for a biscuit, he said, "I hope you ain't expectin' to win against a coal company—hard to do in Logan County."

"I'll win this one. They have no legal right to take my property," Genna said defiantly.

"Might take a lot of money."

"I've got a lot of money."

"Well, good luck to you then," Ben said.

Genna enjoyed the short drive into Logan. She smiled when she thought how these curving roads would have frustrated Lance, but she was in no hurry. She stuck her head out of the window occasionally to look straight up at the mountain tops. Huge rock outcroppings crisscrossed the forested peaks.

The first store she entered she found a navy blue

suit with a rose silk blouse that instantly transformed her into a businesswoman. She wasn't so lucky at the shoe store across the street, but she finally settled on a pair of navy high-heeled sandals. It had been so long since she'd chosen clothing by herself that she felt odd handing money to the aged salesman.

She became aware that several pairs of eyes behind the counter were watching her keenly.

"Aren't you Genna Ross?" one young saleswoman said. "I went to your concert the other night."

"Yes," she answered slowly.

"We thought you'd already gone," the older man said. "Are you going to have another appearance in the area? My grandson wanted to hear you sing."

"No, I have some business to transact here this morning, but I plan to leave in a few days."

After accommodating a shy request from the young woman for an autograph, as well as one for the salesman's grandson, Genna excused herself quickly. She knew she would have to hurry to make it to the law office on time. George Blankenship was waiting for her, as she suspected, his briefcase in hand.

"We're to meet Sullivan and his lawyer at the judge's chambers. I have all of the tax receipts and a copy of your deed. Whoever drew that mining plat made a mistake."

Genna heard only one thing he said. "Sullivan?"

"Yes, Evan Sullivan bought the Keystone Mining Company a few months ago, although it's not generally known. He was forced into strip mining when several of his underground mines played out."

Genna's throat and tongue felt suddenly parched. She swallowed with difficulty. Her knees trembled, and she took the lawyer's arm for support as they climbed the steps to the second floor of the courthouse. She didn't want to make an enemy of Evan, but still she felt angry. *Didn't he remember how Grandpap had felt about strip miners? He seemed to have forgotten other things, but surely he could have remembered that.*

At the end of a narrow hallway, Blankenship stepped aside to allow Genna to enter the room first. Evan and another man, presumably his lawyer, stood facing them. Genna took one quick look and lowered her eyes. She breathed a prayer of thankfulness for the slight warning that Evan was her adversary.

Blankenship shook hands with Evan and his lawyer. "Gentlemen, this is my client, Genevieve Wooten, whose stage name is Genna Ross."

"I've met her," Evan said stonily. His unfriendly voice startled Genna so much that she felt faint. *Had she come back to Logan County for this*?

A door at the rear of the room opened and the judge entered. He motioned them to be seated and joined them at the table.

Turning to Blankenship, he said, "I've studied the case slightly, but you may present your client's position now."

Blankenship stood. “I represent Genevieve Wooten who owns fifty acres of land that once belonged to her grandfather. Mr. Sullivan’s firm, the Keystone Mining Company, has erroneously included this property in its operations on Mill Creek. Apparently, he had bought some land for nonpayment of taxes and thought the Wooten land was included.”

“When that plat was drawn, my client didn’t know that Miss Wooten still owned the land in question, Your Honor,” asserted Keystone’s lawyer.

“I have affidavits and receipts showing that the taxes on that property have never been in arrears,” Blankenship continued. “Even if Mr. Sullivan owns the land adjoining the Wooten property, we want his operations delayed until a survey is made of the line and a fence built to avoid any infringement on my client’s property.”

“But that will take months!” Evan exploded. His lawyer placed a hand on his arm.

“We are willing to concede,” his lawyer stated, “that a mistake was made by the Keystone Company in mapping the property to be mined. We apologize to Miss Wooten and are willing to pay for any inconvenience we may have caused her. The mistake occurred because the Wooten land had at one time belonged to the coal company from which my client bought the property.” Addressing Blankenship, he said, “We are willing to buy her acreage.”

Blankenship looked at Genna, and she shook her head. “The property is not for sale,” Blankenship answered.

"Then would you consider granting a right of way through your property? That hollow is the key to the whole area. If we have to start operations from the east side, it will cause weeks of delay."

"No right of way, and the fence has to be built," Genna said weakly, but she turned to Evan, her voice pleading. "Don't you see? I promised Grandpap. You know how he hated strip mining, how he hated to see the mountains scraped bare. He made me promise that I'd never let that happen to his land. Don't you see?" she repeated. "He's the one who gave me a chance in life. I have to do this." Genna could feel Blankenship's stare but she needed to make Evan understand why she couldn't give in.

Evan jumped to his feet. "All I can see is that you've finally found a way to get even with me. All right, have your revenge, I hope you enjoy it." He kicked his chair away from the desk and headed for the door.

Genna and the two lawyers stared silently after him until the judge rapped on the table.

"Mr. Sullivan, do you want to be cited for contempt of court? Come back here and sit down. These proceedings will close when I say so."

Evan stopped in his tracks. Genna heard him returning, but she didn't look at him.

"I apologize, Your Honor."

"I'm unable to give a decision immediately without studying the facts, but on the surface, it appears that the plaintiff is in her rights. Both parties will be notified as soon as possible. In the meantime, the Keystone Mining operations in the vicinity of Mill Creek will be halted." He stood up and left the room without further comment.

"Evan," Genna whispered, but he didn't look her way. With a face as white and as stony as Pinnacle Rock itself, he rushed through the doorway.

Genna followed Blankenship silently back to his office.

"I'm sure you have nothing to worry about. The judge is fair, and there couldn't possibly be any decision except in your favor," Blankenship said as he sat behind his desk. Genna leaned against a chair, wanting to leave Logan County behind her as quickly as possible. First she would need to settle with the lawyer for his fee. She'd telephone Ivy and Ben that she was leaving and then head for Nashville. Perhaps the fast pace of her personal appearances would deaden the gnawing pain pulling at her heartstrings. She felt the blood drain from her face at Blankenship's next words.

"I feel sorry for Sullivan though. This will probably ruin him."

"What do you mean?"

She eased into a chair, unable to stand any longer.

"He's had his share of reverses—costly strikes and the closing of his bigger mines. He's invested a great deal of capital in this new mining enterprise and his notes are due soon. He has to mine coal or he won't be able to meet his payments. This delay may force him into bankruptcy."

Suddenly, without warning, Genna laid her head down on the desk top and sobbed.

"I supposed he had plenty of money. The Sullivans were always considered rich. I don't want to cause him to lose his business."

"What can you do unless you allow him to strip your property?"

She shook her head. "Anything but that. Can't you contact his lawyer and find out the amount of his debts, or at least what he needs for these next payments? I'd gladly pay off the loans without having him know. If you can make arrangements, I'll have my accountant in Nashville wire the money to you."

"If I can't manage without Sullivan knowing, what then?"

"Then try to persuade him to accept for old times' sake. He was once a . . . friend of mine. I don't want him hurt. I'm going to leave today, but I'll telephone on Friday to see what you've managed."

Genna hurried to the Mercedes, looking up and down the street to be sure she wouldn't encounter Evan. She received a jolt when a young man shoved a video camera in front of her. "We've been waiting for you, Miss Ross," his companion said. "How about an interview?"

"Why not?" Genna shrugged her shoulders. She no longer had a need for anonymity in Logan County.

"It's a surprise to all of us, Miss Ross, that you're from this area. When did you leave here?"

"When my grandfather died about ten years ago. This is my first trip back."

"You've always kept your past a secret—that's been one of your charms. Why did you return now?"

"I wanted to do that benefit show because my grandfather had black lung disease. I'm not ashamed of my roots, although I don't suppose it would have helped my career to advertise that I was an illegitimate child raised by my grandfather, the local moonshiner."

The cameraman kept his instrument tightly focused on Genna's face, as the reporter hurriedly consulted his notepad.

"But why are you revealing this now?"

"I don't much care now who knows. Please excuse me." Still distraught, she slipped into the car and turned the ignition key.

I wonder how long it will be before Jim finds out? she thought with the first traces of amusement she'd felt all day.

six

Even after hours in a Nashville salon transforming herself from Veevie Wooten to Genna Ross, Genna knew the process wasn't a success. She wasn't the same woman she'd been when she departed two weeks ago. In late afternoon she telephoned her staff to set up a dinner meeting. By the sound of Jim's voice Genna knew the media had done their job.

Jim was waiting for her when she entered the lobby of her hotel apartment. "Our table is ready," he said stiffly, holding the door open into the private dining room the hotel had reserved for them. "Lori and Cary are waiting for us."

Genna silently preceded him into the room. The sight of Cary was a balm for her troubled mind, and she bent to kiss her on the cheek. She squeezed Lori's hand.

"Hi, gang! I've missed you. Have you slave drivers scheduled lots of work for me now that my little vacation is over?" she asked brightly.

"There's a recording session at ten in the morning," Jim said as he held her chair. "They're going to use your new song, 'Why Do I Love Him?' as the title number on the new video."

"Oh, that's great!"

They talked of trivia while the waiters brought their food, served family style. When the four of them were alone again, Jim blurted out, "Genna, I'm your manager, but you'd never know it by your actions of the last week. If you have any startling news to release, I'd appreciate if you would tell me first."

"You can believe this or not, I don't care, but I had no intention of revealing anything when I left you in Woodville. I only intended to visit my old homeplace and see two cousins who had no idea I was Genna Ross. Then things just went haywire and people began to recognize me."

"You should have known they would," Lori said, her brown eyes sparkling angrily as she flipped back her long black hair.

She's getting as bad as Jim, Genna thought. *When will these two people realize that they're working for me?*

"Why are you so upset, Jim?" Genna asked, ignoring Lori. "Are you mad because I hadn't told you all, or because you think my past will hurt my success?"

"It won't do you any good."

"I'm not so sure about that," Cary commented quietly. "I thought Lori said the video sales had boomed since that news hit the national networks."

Jim gave her a dirty look.

"Oh, well, forget it!" Genna said. "If there is any harm, it's too late to undo, and I don't want to talk about it. My childhood wasn't so happy that I like to recall it, so let's finish our meal without an argument. Seems like that's all we do anymore."

The next day after two hours in the recording studio for her new video, Genna stopped at a deli for a sandwich and an iced tea.

"To go," she told the young clerk, who looked at her with admiring eyes. When Genna left the store she caught sight of Jim a block away running to catch up with her.

"Wait up," Jim called, "I'll grab a sandwich, and we'll go over your contract with Soundtone Recordings while we eat."

"No, Jim, I need a break from shop talk."

"You've been gone for two weeks. What more do you want?"

"I need to be by myself for a while. I'll be at my apartment at two o'clock. Why don't you come by then?" She exited through the sliding door into the parking garage.

Dodging the noonday traffic, she was soon on Interstate 40 heading eastward. She rolled down the window and let the wind blow freely through her hair. Even though the recording had gone well, she'd been under stress and found it difficult to relax in Nashville where so many people knew her. Those few days in the mountains had given her a taste of solitude, and she missed it.

Genna left the interstate at the first interchange beyond the city's limits. She drove aimlessly for a half-hour on a state highway then turned off on a narrow road. She passed many small farms, admiring the fields of ripened corn that awaited the picker. As she approached a small brick church situated on a knoll above the road, she noticed a picnic shelter on the oak-shaded lawn nearby and she pulled into the vacant parking lot.

She nibbled at the sandwich while enjoying the antics of two squirrels. They scurried around the lawn collecting acorns that they then carried to some secluded spot in the high trees. Genna tried to interest them in bits of her sandwich, but the squirrels sniffed indifferently, swished their tails, and hurried off to gather more nuts. The squawking bluejays greedily grabbed the tidbits the squirrels rejected.

After disposing of the paper bag in a trash can, she wandered into the tiny church cemetery, still loathe to return to Nashville. Glancing at her watch, she knew she had to leave or be late for her appointment with Jim.

She had just reached the car when a huge bus drove into the parking lot. "CAROL SUE AND THE HOSANNAS" was brightly painted across both sides of the bus.

Carol Sue? The name sounded familiar and Genna hesitated. The bus door opened and a spritely brunette hurried down the steps.

"Hi," she called to Genna, as she breathed in the air scented with drying hay from the nearby fields. "What a beautiful day!"

"And what a beautiful woman!" Genna laughingly answered.

The woman flashed her a smile. "Thanks." She eyed Genna keenly. "Should I know you?"

"Maybe. Genna Ross sound familiar?"

"Sure. I saw your picture in the recording studio

this morning. You were recording in Studio B. I was across the hall."

"Let's hope our tapes didn't get mixed up."

"Yes, let's! I'm afraid my public might be disillusioned if 'One-Man Woman' became crossed with 'Amazing Grace.'"

"Oh, so you're a gospel singer. I remember you now. Aren't you the rock star who turned to gospel music a few years ago?"

"Yes, and those few years have been the happiest time of my life. I'd like to tell you about it sometime."

"I'd love to hear it," Genna said earnestly, stirred by the radiance of her brief witness.

"Are you coming to the concert tonight? I always give a testimony sometime during the evening."

"Where is the concert? Here?"

"Yes," Carol Sue said with a grin, "and from the size of this building, we may have to hold the concert in the parking lot."

With her heart still heavy and her thoughts still clouded, Genna sped back into town to keep her appointment with Jim. As usual, he had a list of schedules for her to look over.

"I've got two surprises for you," he said, smiling suavely. "Wait until you see your December schedule."

"Europe!" Genna exclaimed, excitement brightening her eyes. "You managed it at last."

"Yes, your last concert stateside is in Columbus, Ohio, November 29th. After that, we'll be flying to

London for a week's tour in the British Isles."

"And I'll have appearances at several American military bases on the continent, I see."

"We'll finish the last concert December 20th, in plenty of time to be home for Christmas."

"I see this schedule goes through March 31st. Don't make any other commitments after that for two or three months. I'll do the fairs in August and September, but nothing in the spring months."

"Why not?"

"I have other plans."

"I'm waiting breathlessly."

Genna stood up indicating the interview was over.

"The other surprise can wait. I can't stand too much good news at once. Is there anything else you need to discuss with me?"

His eyes glittered angrily, and he obviously struggled with an angry retort.

"Yes, I'd like to discuss dinner tonight. Any objections to going out with me?"

"None at all. In fact, I even have a place I want you to take me after we've eaten."

"Just using me for a chauffeur?"

"Forget it then. I don't need an escort. I'll go alone or ask Lance."

"No, no, I'll take you."

"Good. I'll be ready at five o'clock. If you'll excuse me, Lori is due in a few minutes, and we have a lot of correspondence to deal with."

"I just can't figure you out. You've been different ever since we played that one-horse town in

West Virginia. Have you found another man?"

"Honestly, Jim, I haven't found the first one yet!" *Must she tell him in plain English that she was tired of his possessiveness*? He was a good manager—why couldn't he be content with that?

Genna assessed Jim's potential a few hours later seated across from him in the seafood restaurant. He was on his best behavior and Genna sincerely wished she could care for him. Had Evan thwarted her ability to love? Now after ten years, did she truly love Evan or was she still in love with what they once had?

"Since you've told the press about your childhood, I can't see any reason why you can't share it with me," Jim commented.

Genna shrugged her shoulders. "Not really so much to tell, I reckon. I was an illegitimate child, and my mother died giving birth to me. My grandparents took me in and raised me."

"Unwanted child and all that, huh? A real tear-jerker."

His tone offended her, but she tried to push aside her resentment. "No, I can't say I ever felt unwanted. They were good to me, and Grandpap was especially loving after my grandmother died. He saved enough to provide me with an education when I went to California to live with my cousin."

"What about his being a moonshiner?"

"Lots of people make moonshine in Logan County—a perfectly respectable occupation, some think."

"You know the more I hear about this, the more I

think it would make a great book and movie. People love to read about and see these heartbreaking, rags to riches stories."

"No, Jim. I would never agree to it, so let's say no more. I don't want my family's name dragged through the mud. No book. No movie."

"Okay, okay! It was just a thought." He threw up his hands. "Where are we going tonight?"

"To a gospel concert by Carol Sue and the Hosannas."

He uttered a loud guffaw. "You've got to be kidding." A quick glance at the expression on her face told him she had never been more serious. "Wait a minute. Are you getting religion? Is that what's wrong with you?"

Nettled, she replied, "There's nothing wrong with me. And I've always been religious."

"Oh, I know you've always been straight enough, but don't spring any of this spiritual jazz on me."

Genna gathered her purse. "Unless you want dessert, let's go. The concert starts in less than an hour, and we have several miles to drive."

The little brick church was crowded with people but Genna and Jim managed to wedge into a seat near the front.

Because Genna seldom attended concerts other than her own, she immediately became interested in the audience and the effect the music had on them. The audience seemed to have come from all over as most people were strangers to each other. Thankfully, she and Jim didn't create any undue interest.

Other than the type of music, she couldn't see that the concert differed much from hers. Three women, the Hosannas, sang background music to most of the star's songs. Carol Sue was dressed in sequined garments, and her band was much like the one that traveled with Genna. The big difference was in the message of the music.

When Carol Sue sang about the cross and the love of God, Genna traveled back to her childhood. There was Miss Amelia, sitting at the piano of Bethel Church, a group of children gathered around singing. She remembered especially the lyrics, "What a friend we have in Jesus, all our sins and griefs to bear."

Had that been why she'd been able to stand Evan's unfaithfulness and the loss of Grandpap? When Carol Sue sang, "He was there all the time," Genna wondered how ever-present God had been in her life. All the time when she shifted from West Virginia to California? All the time when she went to college? All the time when she was on her rise to fame? Had He been there all the time, and she hadn't been conscious of it?

Genna realized her palms were moist and she suddenly felt faint. *He'd been there, and she hadn't recognized Him.*

During intermission Genna visited the women's room while Jim searched for some refreshments. Returning to the church's sanctuary, Genna came face to face with Carol Sue.

"So you did come!"

"Yes, and it's a great show." The lights blinked that intermission was almost over and Carol Sue turned to leave. "Let's talk sometime," she called over her shoulder.

The second half started with several numbers from Carol Sue's latest album. When it was time for the inspirational closing, the lights dimmed and Carol Sue stood spotlighted, the three Hosannas humming softly in the background.

"As you know, I had a startling run of successes in the rock music field," she began. "My career started at sixteen, and by the time I was twenty, I'd reached the top. There was nothing wrong with my rock music. It was clean, and it appealed to a vast audience. I enjoyed doing it, but one day something happened to me. I met my Master face to face."

A chorus of "Amens" amid wild applause interrupted her testimony. Jim glanced at Genna, a hint of exasperation on his face. "Let's get out of here. These people are nuts."

She silenced him with a brusque wave of her hand.

"And once I'd met the Master, everything I'd achieved paled into insignificance. For two years, I've been singing to praise Him, spreading His name around the world. I have a new audience, a new set of fans, but more importantly, I have a peace in my heart that the world can't take away. The Bible promises, 'And the peace of God, which transcends all understanding, will guard your hearts and your minds in Christ Jesus.' I've found that peace, and I pray that you will too."

I had that peace once and I want it again, Genna thought. *The resentment I've harbored against Evan has been a barrier to my spiritual growth.*

She shook her head and tried to concentrate on the woman on stage. As the lights brightened, Carol Sue said, "We have a special guest in the audience tonight, and if none of you has met her, this would be a good time. Genna Ross, will you come forward, please?"

Genna felt Jim physically sinking into his seat, and he mumbled through clinched teeth, "Now look what you've done." She blithely ignored him and made her way to the stage amid a wave of applause.

"How about doing a number with me?" Carol Sue whispered as the applause faded.

Startled, Genna said, "Carol Sue, what would we sing? I don't know any of your favorites."

"Think of something you know and we'll give it a try. You sing the lead, and I'll fill in on the harmony."

Again, Genna thought of Bethel Church and Miss Amelia's favorite chorus, "I've Got the Joy, Joy, Joy, down in My Heart."

Genna hummed a measure of the chorus. "Do you know that one? The second verse fits in with what you've said tonight."

Nodding, Carol Sue said a few words to the band, and the two women swung into the old chorus.

" 'I've got the peace that passeth understanding

down in my heart, down in my heart, down in my heart. I've got the peace that passeth understanding down in my heart, down in my heart to stay.' "

Carol Sue held up her hands to acknowledge the enthusiastic applause. "Thanks, folks. Maybe we can do this again sometime." She hugged Genna. "Let's keep in touch."

Jim hardly spoke all the way back to Nashville, and Genna was too involved in the new sensations of her spirit to even care. Finally, she broke the silence by laughing.

"It isn't funny, Genna. Things like this can ruin your career."

"Oh, be realistic, Jim. I had no idea this was going to happen. I met Carol Sue today and she invited me to the concert. I went out of curiosity. I didn't suppose she'd even know I was there, but I happened to meet her during intermission."

"As your manager, I'm supposed to keep things from 'happening' to you, but I can't do it when you're determined to go your own way. We need to be in control of your future, not just let it run along haphazardly."

"Jim, for the first time in years, I'm beginning to think that I'm not in control of my future. There may be something more ahead than I know about."

"What do you mean by that?" he demanded.

"I don't know myself. When I have it figured out, I'll let you know."

"Please do," he said sarcastically.

When they reached the door of her apartment, she looked at her watch. "There's time for you to come in and tell me about the second surprise you mentioned."

Genna filled two glasses with soft drinks and set a tray of veggies and crackers on the coffee table. Jim picked up his glass and drained it and asked for a refill before he removed some brochures from his jacket pocket and handed them to Genna.

"A representative from this company approached me last week with the proposition to produce a new line of jewelry known as the Genna Ross Collection. What's your opinion?"

Genna smiled. "I'm certainly willing to talk to them about it but I'll reserve my final opinion until I know more details. Why don't you make an appointment with their representative?"

Since Genna had worn the firm's jewelry, she had no reluctance to put her name on their products. The company had been in business for over fifty years and had earned a well-deserved reputation of quality workmanship. As they discussed the idea, Genna and Jim agreed that the project would be advantageous. The ease of their conversation reminded Genna of the working relationship she and Jim had once had, and perhaps could have again.

Before she prepared for bed, Genna opened the safe in the bedroom where some of her jewelry was stored. Her hand trembled when she sorted out a tattered cardboard box from among the many velvet containers. She lifted a white opal ring from the box and held it to her lips. It had been months since she'd looked at the ring, the gift from Evan on her sixteenth birthday. She had worn the ring on a chain around her neck until three years ago when its fragile band had broken in two. The ring had been repaired, but Genna had not worn it again. Although the gold needed to be polished, the opal still displayed its rainbow of colors. She slipped it on her finger and slid the band back and forth enjoying the brilliance of the fiery stone. Genna had never owned another opal.

That night Genna went to sleep with the ring on her hand. Memories of Pinnacle Mountain filtered through her dreams, the wind shifting the leaves, dappled rays of sunshine painting the rock where she and Evan sat.

When she met with the jewelry company's representative two days later, Genna liked his proposition. She would have final approval on any new item added to the line, and she'd receive a ten percent royalty on all sales.

"I've been thinking about this," Genna said, "and I do have one stipulation to make before we proceed any further. I want an opal on every piece of jewelry that bears the Genna Ross name."

"But opals are out of fashion now," Jim objected. "Very few people buy them."

"The Genna Ross name will sell them. Besides, it's a lovely stone that should be revived."

The representative was silent for several minutes and then smiled shrewdly. "Miss Ross, you've just come up with a great suggestion. We haven't been able to agree on a name for the line yet, but I can see great possibilities with the opal as our centerpiece. It will run the price up higher than we had anticipated— we'd buy only the best gemstones, the black opals of South Wales and the white opals of Australia and Europe." He paused for effect, then added excitedly, "We could call the line 'Opal Fire.' I can't speak for all of the management, but with your permission, I'm going to recommend it."

After he left, Jim looked at Genna. "How did you come up with that idea?"

"I've always liked opals."

"You don't *have* any opals."

"Not any you've seen, but I'll wager I'll be wearing lots of them now. 'Opal Fire'—I like that name."

seven

"Our last stop before Europe," Cary said as she arranged Genna's hair for the performance that night at the municipal auditorium in Columbus, Ohio.

"I'll be glad for a few days' rest before we head overseas. This has been a rugged year in many ways."

"But a good year, too, dear," Cary reminded her. Besides Genna's sold-out concert tour, advance sales of the Opal Fire jewelry collection had already exceeded a million dollars and the line wouldn't be ready for distribution until March.

Genna felt like someone with a split personality. Onstage, she was still Genna Ross, the country western sensation, but during her quiet times, Veevie Wooten, the simple country girl, was dominant. On those days she longed for the the quietness of the hollow on a dew-spangled morning, the exhilarating walk to Pinnacle Rock, and the comfort of being with her own kind. Could a mountaineer ever be completely happy away from the hills? When the land of your birth tugged at your heartstrings, would you ever feel in complete harmony elsewhere?

This latest bout of melancholy had been sparked by a dated communique from George Blankenship. Blankenship had written six weeks earlier, and although the letter had been forwarded twice, it had reached her only yesterday.

"I want you to know I have used your money to bail out the Keystone Mining Company," Blankenship had written. "The gift was offered anonymously, per your instructions. The surveyor marked the boundary between your land and that purchased by Keystone. A fence has been built around your farm. The mountain is being stripped now, and I can understand your loathing of the project. Although Sullivan has guaranteed to reclaim the land, as of this letter the mountain is nothing but an eyesore."

New thoughts of Evan had surfaced with the letter as well as the debut of her new song that night, "Why Do I Love Him?" Every time she sang the heartwrenching lyrics, Evan's face floated across her thoughts. Not coincidentally, the Columbus concert was scheduled for the same day as the release of the video and album based on the song. When Genna ran onstage to the thunderous applause of her fans, the band gave the cue and she swung into the lyrics.

When he's unfaithful, or cold or far away,
I still love that man of mine.
Even though my heart, he once betrayed
I'll love him for all time.
Why do I love him?
I don't always know,
But it isn't any secret that . . .
He's the dawn of my morning,
The heat of the noonday sun;

He's the warmth of late evening,
My strength when the day is done.

Genna's eyes misted at the applause of the enthusiastic audience. Amid the chanting demands for an encore, her heart cried, "Oh, Evan, Evan!"

After intermission, dressed in the garb of a mountain woman, Genna picked up her lap dulcimer and, as usual, presented a selection of mountain folk songs. When the last echoes of applause had died in the back rows, Genna's next selections surprised even herself. Almost as if her fingers moved of their own volition, she swung into a medley of hymns beginning with "Amazing Grace" and "What a Friend We Have in Jesus." Although the band faltered a time or two, they were good at following her lead. By the time she concluded with "God Be With You Til We Meet Again," the band's accompaniment was as polished as ever.

Jim might quarrel with her, but her audience, after its first startled silence, interrupted her singing time and again with applause. *I'll make this a part of every concert,* she thought, feeling in her heart that this was right for her.

Ater the third curtain call, she finally surrendered to the demands of her insistent fans with a stirring rendition of "One-Man Woman."

Blowing kisses at the crowd, she escaped at last to her dressing room.

"Did you hear the concert, Cary?" Genna asked as she began removing her stage makeup.

"Yes, it's one of your best. I liked the gospel music and so did the audience."

"I haven't seen Jim yet, but I can guess his reaction."

"He'll like anything that will roll in proceeds at the box office and increase his bonus. Jim has two great ambitions in life—to become a rich, rich man, and you know what the other is."

"The first ambition he may achieve; the other, he won't."

She disappeared into the shower, and came out with a belted pink terrycloth robe. She relaxed on Cary's padded table for her postconcert massage.

"I've never bothered you with questions, Genna, but I wonder why he won't?"

"Won't what? Oh, you mean, Jim's ambition? I . . . ." A knock on the door interrupted her.

"Who is it?" Cary asked.

"Message for Miss Ross," a male voice answered.

Cary shielded Genna behind a slightly opened door. A hand holding a small envelope reached through the opening. "I'm to wait for an answer," the voice said.

Genna glanced at the writing before she opened the envelope. The script had a slightly familiar look.

Veevie (you're still that to me),
I attended your concert tonight.
May I see you?
Evan

Genna suddenly felt unbearably warm and her hand trembled as she handed the note back to Cary.

"That's the reason."

Cary scanned the message. "I don't understand."

"That's the reason Jim will never realize his ambition."

"Oh," Cary said softly.

"But you needn't advertise that fact. Where's a pen?"

Silently, Cary found one in her purse. Genna paused indecisively for a few moments before she scribbled, "Yes. My dressing room, five minutes."

She scrambled off the table and glanced in the mirror. Her hair streaming down her back and her face devoid of cosmetics, she looked like the Veevie of long ago.

"We don't have much time," Cary said. "What clothes do you want to wear? Do you want me to do your hair?"

Genna wrapped the robe closely around her. "There's no time for my hair. Let me just slip into the pants and sweater I wore here tonight." With years of experience as a quick-change artist, Genna was ready when Evan knocked softly two times.

Cary opened the door and slipped into the adjoining room as he entered. Facing Evan from across the room, the distance seemed as wide as an ocean to Genna.

After a long silence, she spoke first. "And I always thought I'd know if you ever attended one of my performances!"

"I was traveling through town on my way home from Detroit when I heard the announcement of your concert on a local radio station. Impulsively, I decided to attend. At first I thought I'd go on and not let you know I'd been here. I was afraid you'd turn me down if I asked to see you."

With her throat tight and painful, Genna shook her head and whispered, "Never."

"I won't stay long. I just wanted you to know I thought you were great. No wonder Michelle raves about you. I'll have to listen to your tapes; she has enough of them."

"Is that the only reason you came?" The strength of his presence overwhelmed her. Genna Ross had fled; she was all Veevie Wooten now, a woman who loved this man wholeheartedly.

"I forfeited my right to anything more a long time ago."

With her eyes never leaving his, she began to sing softly.

No other man will claim me for life,
No other man can make me his wife,
Only one man will win my heart . . .
For I've been a one-man woman right from the start.

In two quick moves, Evan crossed the room and gathered her into his arms. His heart beat rapidly, keeping time with her own pulsebeat.

"My Veevie, I wouldn't presume, wouldn't dare to hope, that you were singing about me after what

I've done to you."

He lowered his head until she could feel his warm breath on her face. A knock sounded at the door.

"Who is it?" she demanded irritably.

"Jim and Lori. Are you ready for dinner?"

She drifted out of Evan's arms whispering, "Do you have to leave right away?"

"I'm driving home tonight, but I can delay a few more hours. I want to talk to you, Veevie."

Genna opened the door and Jim and Lori breezed in. They stopped in surprise at the sight of Evan. Genna Ross wasn't in the habit of admitting fans to her dressing room.

"Jim, Lori, meet a friend of mine, Evan Sullivan. Evan, this is my manager and secretary."

If he ever had any good manners, Jim forgot them now. "Where in thunder did you drop from? I've never heard of you."

Evan's face flushed angrily, but without waiting for him to answer, Genna said, "Evan is an old friend, and we have lots to talk about. I'm having dinner with him so the two of you can go ahead without me."

She stood by the door they hadn't bothered to close and motioned them out.

Jim paused in the doorway. "What time will you be back? I have some details about Opal Fire to discuss with you."

Just to annoy him, she said, "We can talk after breakfast."

He exited without another word and Genna said,

"Pardon me for inviting myself to dinner, but sometimes Jim's protective role is a bit hard to take."

Evan rubbed his chin. "I'm not sure protective is the right word, but I'll be delighted to take you to dinner."

"Good. I'll tell Cary where I'm going."

In the adjoining room, she quickly summoned Cary with a look of excited desperation. "Think you can do my hair real fast, Cary?"

"He can wait a few minutes," Cary said with a laugh.

"Maybe, but I can't. I've waited twelve years for a date with him."

Cary brushed her hair, and with a few quick turns of the curling iron brought the unruly tresses under control. "Please pack my things, Cary, so they can be stored on the bus. I'll see you at the hotel."

"My car is down the street in a parking garage," Evan said when she joined him. "Do you have any place in mind to eat?"

"No, you choose. I eat very little on a concert day so I'm ravenous now."

She'd forgotten how broad and powerful he was. As a young man, Evan had been tall and slender, but the years had fleshed him out until he seemed to dwarf her. Strength seemed to radiate from him.

When he left the traffic behind, heading westward, he said, "I've wanted to apologize for the way I treated you the last time we met, Genna.

Guess I'd better get used to calling you that," he added slowly, "but I like Veevie better."

With a smile, she touched his arm. "Do you mean you like Veevie better than Genna as a person or as a name?"

"I thought Veevie was more approachable. I was never afraid of her—I'm uncomfortable with Genna."

"I haven't changed that much, Evan. The outside trappings are different but inwardly I'm much the same."

He squeezed her hand. "I hope so. I'm sorry I was so belligerent that day in Logan, but I was on the brink of ruin, and I couldn't stand to think that you'd be the one who would finally send me there. Maybe I deserved it from you, but it hurt to think you were being vindictive. Since then, I've had time to appreciate your side of the case."

"Evan, I had no idea you owned the Keystone Company until a few minutes before we came to that courthouse. I had no choice anyway—you know how Grandpap felt about strip mining."

"Yes, I remember. But I was so excited about seeing you again, and then to find out that you were the party opposing me was more than I could take."

"Are things going better now?"

"Yes, I had a surprise reprieve, and now that I've started more mining operations, I'm coming out of the financial slump. That worry is over, but I have another one facing me."

"Oh?"

"The union at the deep mine is pushing for benefits that I can't afford. The miners' contract runs out in January, and I'm sure they'll strike. If they wait for me to meet their demands, they might as well."

"I'm sorry, Evan. You've had your problems."

"And they all started when I lost you."

"I hardly think it's accurate to say you lost me. You simply shoved me away."

"Ouch! I know that's true, but I tried to explain to you about that."

"Regardless, I don't want to talk about the past, Evan. It's too painful. Tell me what you're doing now. Tell me about your daughter."

"Michelle is eight years old now, and we're great friends."

"Do you have any help with her?"

"Yes, I have a housekeeper. I'm gone too much to have Michelle at home alone. Mrs. Gilley is about fifty years old and has a solid head on her shoulders. She's able to command Michelle's respect and friendship."

"That sounds like a good combination."

"Michelle is going with her maternal grandparents to Florida for the Christmas holidays, and since that will leave me footloose, I've decided to take a vacation. Anything's better than spending Christmas alone worrying about the strike."

"Where are you going?"

"To the Holy Land. All my life I've dreamed of being in Bethlehem on Christmas Eve. I want to walk out in the open and see the stars as they must have shone the night Jesus was born."

"That sounds like a fine vacation. Circumstances aren't quite so tense in the Middle East now."

Evan slowed the car. "I don't know much about this area, but that sign indicates the next interchange has some restaurants. Shall we stop there?"

"Sure. I don't care where we eat."

The area didn't offer much choice, but they finally decided on a steakhouse. Evan bowed his head over the food, and Genna prayed too. It had been a long time since she'd been so thankful.

"Considering all the things that have happened to you, I'm surprised you ever thought of me. Why didn't you forget me entirely? You had every right." Evan looked deeply into her eyes.

"I tried to, Evan. I didn't like to live with resentment, but more than that, I didn't want to hold on to a dream."

"Do you still feel that way, Genna? Haven't you ever forgiven me?"

"I think so, Evan. The trouble is that I'm afraid of love now. I don't want to be hurt again."

He squeezed her hand. "I'm sorry for what I did. Is there any way I can make it up to you now?"

"Not unless you can help me forget the past."

"We can do that by talking about the present. What are your plans?"

"The greatest thing for me in the future is a trip to Europe during December. Jim has tried to arrange an overseas tour for a long time. We leave New York next week, and that will give me time to rest a bit after ten days of nightly performances."

"You like this life style?"

"Yes, it gets in your blood. You live from one concert to the next. It's been good therapy for me."

They left the restaurant shortly before midnight. "I wish you didn't have that long drive. I shouldn't have asked you to stay, but a few minutes together didn't seem like enough."

He drew her close to his side when they entered the car. "This evening has meant more to me than you'll ever know. Thinking about it will keep me from going to sleep."

The return drive passed quickly and they were back in the city sooner than Genna anticipated. She wasn't ready to say goodbye yet. What about the future? Or was there any future for them?

Evan walked with her to the door of her room. "Genna, is it possible for us to forget the past and start over? I don't want to walk away without some plan to see you again. Is there still a place for me in your life?"

"I hope so, Evan. I hope so," she whispered. "Why don't you telephone me before we leave for Europe? I'll be at the Roosevelt Hotel in New York next week."

"Depend on it."

They faced one another as if yearning for a youthful love that they would never share again. Genna felt like a teenager waiting for her first kiss. Would Evan make the first move? She doubted it, but she couldn't.

She extended her hand, but Evan ignored it and drew her into a tight embrace. She nestled against him breathing in his presence. In his arms, she sensed the fragrance of the wild plum trees blooming in the creek valley. She smelled the smoke from the coal burning in Grandpap's fireplace as she and Evan had stared into the embers and dreamed of the future. So much of her past belonged to Evan.

Genna lifted her lips and Evan needed no other invitation. The past receded and she was overcome by new sensations. Nothing she'd ever experienced before with him compared to the longing she now felt. The youthful Veevie had never known what it was like to have every nerve flaming at the touch of his lips. The adult woman Genna wasn't sure she liked her reaction. She would never allow Evan to hurt her again, but in his arms she was vulnerable.

Genna pulled away quickly. "It's time for you to go."

Evan laughed huskily and his voice was unsteady. "Yes, I guess I should. I'll call you next weekend. Goodbye, Genna."

eight

Sensing Genna's reluctance to be alone with Jim, Cary stayed close to her the next day. But Jim wasn't to be thwarted so easily. When the bus entered Pennsylvania and picked up speed on Interstate 80, Jim made his move. "Genna, I want to talk to you alone." Sluggishly Genna left the seat beside Cary and strolled back to the office where Lori was typing fan letters for her signature. "Would you excuse us now, Lori?" Jim said.

Lori gave him a resentful look and left without a word.

"Now, who is the big guy?" Jim said as soon as they were alone.

Genna eyed him levelly as she answered, not once diverting her gaze. "I told you who he was, Evan Sullivan, an old friend."

"How old? How long have you known him? It must have been before I knew you."

"Jim, I'd lived more than twenty years of my life before I met you. I knew hundreds of people in that time. Is it necessary for me to report on everyone?"

"I'm not interested in anyone except Sullivan. How long has it been since you've seen him? Is he the reason you've changed and become so secretive lately?"

Genna glared at him, her thoughts churning. She

wasn't going to submit to this third degree. Jim must be out of his mind to interrogate her in this manner.

"I don't want to fight with you, Genna."

"Then don't do it. You're the antagonist. There's nothing in our contract that says you have control over my personal life, or my professional life for that matter. You work for *me*. Do I have to keep reminding you of that?"

"If you wreck your career—all we've worked for—because of some local yokel, I'll be hurt too. That gives me some right to question you."

Genna laughed at his preposterous statement. "Jim, you've gone from the ridiculous to downright insulting. Stop being foolish. We'd better go over my tour schedule again. If you spend the next three days in Massachusetts with your sister, we won't have another time."

The expression in Jim's eyes was pleading, but Genna ignored it. He didn't resume his interrogation, but his manner remained stiff and unyielding during the rest of the trip.

During their few days in New York, Cary and Genna slept late, breakfasted at leisure in the hotel's coffee shop, lunched in exotic restaurants, and shopped in elegant stores. The Madison Avenue stores were decorated for Christmas and Cary soon became caught up in the infectious spirit.

"Don't buy all of your presents here, Cary," cautioned Genna as Cary's legion of shopping bags threatened to overwhelm passersby. "Remember, you'll have three weeks in Europe. You'll want to buy some things over there."

"But we're always rushed on these tours. You know how Jim exacts every bit of publicity he can. We'll be busy all the time. By the time we return to the States, all of the merchandise will be picked over. I'm looking out for my grandkids now."

"Maybe you're right," Genna conceded, as she and Cary entered yet another fashionable emporium. Ben would like the binoculars she found in an interesting high-tech store, but Ivy would probably shake her head over the shirtwaist silk dress and leave it hanging in the closet. At least, she'd have the exclusive store box and wrapping to show the neighbors.

Even though Genna hummed Christmas carols along with the melodies wafting from loudspeakers throughout the stores, inside she didn't feel like celebrating. Since Bea's death, Genna had spent Christmas alone. The holiday was an unhappy time for her and she was always relieved when it was over. Maybe the European tour would be a help this year.

"What are you doing for Christmas, Genna?" Cary asked one morning at breakfast. "My daughter told me to invite you to spend the holidays with us in Nashville."

Genna shook her head. "Thanks, but I won't do that. Christmas is a family time, and you need to be away from shop talk for a week. I haven't really thought about it. I may stay over a week in Europe. If you're right about Jim keeping us busy, I won't have any time to sightsee, and I'd hate to come home without visiting some of the great landmarks."

"Alone?"

"I'm a big girl, Cary. I don't need anyone to stay with me. You make your plans to go home and forget about me."

Evan's call came two days before they left, much to Genna's relief. Her old fears about him had returned. Genna cuddled the phone lovingly under her chin and for a few minutes they talked of trivial matters.

"What are your plans for Christmas?" he asked.

"I don't have any. My last concert is on the 20th so the band and my staff can arrive stateside in time for Christmas. I may stay in Europe for a few days. I have to be home by January 2nd, Jim has a concert planned in Boston."

"Maybe I shouldn't ask, but will you meet me in Israel for a few days?"

Genna gasped. "Oh, I don't know, Evan."

Insistently, he continued. "I'm going on a group tour, and we'll be in Tel Aviv from the 21st until the 27th. From there we will visit Bethlehem. I'd like to see the Holy Land with you."

"It may be too late to make arrangements."

"You could stay in the same hotel where the tour group is based, and you might even be able to join the tour for a few days. I'm traveling with Watoga Tours. We'll leave Israel for Athens on the 27th, but we could spend some time together before you have to fly home."

"I'll have to think about it, Evan. Let me telephone you tomorrow."

"But tell me, Veevie," he persisted, laughing at his choice of names, "do you want to go? To me, that's almost as important as if you do go."

Genna's answer came after only a slight hesitation.

"Yes, Evan, I want to go very much."

"Good. I'll wait for your call. I love you, Veevie," he whispered softly before he replaced the phone.

Genna lay back on the bed, not realizing that she hadn't replaced the phone receiver until the recorded operator's voice startled her.

Genna considered having Lori check on travel arrangements, but on second thought, she decided to do it herself. She'd prefer that Jim didn't know where she was during that time, and what Lori knew, Jim knew.

The next morning she telephoned Watoga Tours' local office. The salesperson who answered readily said, "Yes, we'll be pleased to have you join our tour at Tel Aviv for three days. Would you like for me to arrange your air passage too?"

"That would be a help. I'll arrive in Israel from Frankfurt, Germany. Will you deliver my travel documents to the Roosevelt Hotel?"

In less than two hours, the woman contacted Genna to assure her that all the scheduling had been completed. Trying to stifle her excitement, she telephoned the news to Evan.

"I'm all set," she said. "I'll be on the Lufthansa flight arriving in Tel Aviv from Frankfurt at 10:30 A.M. on December 22nd. I can join your tour that afternoon."

"Great! That's the best news I've heard in months. It will be good for us, Genna."

"Do I pretend not to know you?"

"Of course not. What gave you such an idea?"

"It might be embarrassing for your tour companions."

"I don't know any of the other people on the tour, but it wouldn't matter anyway. You wouldn't embarrass me."

"Not even if I said 'hit,' 'ain't,' and things like that?"

When he remained silent, Genna wished she'd kept her mouth shut. "No matter what you say," Evan said evenly.

Jim had booked a concert for every night in the British Isles, leaving only one free day before they flew to Germany. His good mood was a reflection of the great reception Genna had received, so he amicably agreed to go with them on a day's tour. "But with only one day to see England, how can we possibly make a choice?" Lori moaned.

"Why don't we all write down the place we most want to see within a day's drive of London? We'll mix them together, draw out one choice, and that's where we'll go," Jim suggested.

Cary's choice of Salisbury Cathedral was the winner and no one seemed disappointed. They rented a van large enough to accommodate their party and hired a guide to ride with them. Though it would rush them to make their nine o'clock flight from Heathrow Airport, they agreed to see Stonehenge as well while they were in the vicinity.

Long before they completed their eighty-mile drive from London, the spire of Salisbury Cathedral greeted their view. The landscape of grassy uplands and rolling plains was mostly devoted to farming and pastureland. Flocks of sheep dotted the green fields.

Their guide, a thirtyish, vivacious English woman with a cockney accent kept up a running commentary as they traveled through the countryside. The driver of the van, Genna's electric guitarist, had no trouble adhering to the left side of the traffic as they entered the little town of Salisbury. They took turns exclaiming over the many Tudor-style inns and tearooms lining the streets. "No place else in England will you find a purer example of the pointed, early English style of architecture than here at Salisbury Cathedral," their guide began when they reached the grounds of the cathedral. "Construction on this edifice started in 1220 and it took thirty-eight years to complete. Workers completed the spire in the fourteenth century.

"I would suggest you visit the cathedral's octagonal Chapter House noted for its fine sculpture dating from the thirteenth century and see one of the four remaining copies of the Magna Carta in the library. Take a look also at the clock in the north transept, reportedly the oldest working mechanism in Europe."

The guide handed brochures to all of them, and when the others walked toward the entrance, Genna took Cary's hand. "Let's walk on the lawn first."

Jim seemed eager to join in step. "I'll go with you."

"No, we'll catch you later." He frowned but didn't tag along as Genna feared he would.

The cathedral sat on a wide, rich lawn atop a level plain beside the gently flowing Avon River. Genna wrapped her coat more closely around her as a keen breeze blew across the plain. The stone of the cathedral had a yellowish sheen in the bright light.

"Hard to believe this building has been standing over 700 years," Cary commented as they walked back toward the cathedral.

Genna smiled. "I feel quite insignificant when I consider the magnificence of the building."

"Don't I hear organ music?"

"I hope so. I'd love to be here during a service."

They hurried into the north transept, pausing to look at the clock the guide had mentioned, and then moved in the direction of the nave. An organ recital was in progress and they quietly slid into a pew. Genna glanced around, amazed to see hundreds of people sitting in rapt attention as the strains of the mighty organ vibrated throughout the building.

When the music ended in about fifteen minutes,

Genna realized how absorbed she'd been in her own thoughts. Again and again she felt confronted with the question, "Where do I go from here?"

After traveling the nine miles north to the renowned Stonehenge, the bus stopped near the large oval of lintels and pillars made from rough-cut stones. Reported to be England's most important ancient monument, Lori was unimpressed with the moment of unveiling. "Fiddle! I thought these things were huge!"

All were irritated because a fence separated them from the famed spot. Nonplussed, the guide said, "You have to use your imagination to realize that these pillars represent a major engineering feat. Most of these stones, some weighing tons, were moved here from some great distance, probably from Wales, 3500 years ago during a time when the ancients had no heavy equipment to help them."

"Why are they considered so important?" one of the young band members questioned. "I've never heard of the place."

"Some historians associate this site with the Druids, while others think it was an astronomical calendar capable of predicting eclipses. But whether it was an ancient burial ground, sun-worshiping temple, or a human sacrifice site, it's still an important remnant of ancient history," the guide said crisply.

"If you say so," the young man said and entered the bus for a nap while the others circled the strange assortment of stones, many of which had toppled from their original spots.

"You're *what*?" Jim shouted. It was the final night of their tour, and he was in her room at Frankfurt.

"I'm not going home with the rest of you tomorrow. I want to do some sightseeing before I go back to the States."

"If you think I'm going to leave you over here alone, you're crazy. Or will you be alone?" he asked suspiciously.

She laughed. Even Jim's churlishness couldn't dampen her pleasure when she was on her way to spend a few days with Evan. Her evident happiness had radiated through her singing and every show had been a beautiful experience.

"No, I won't be alone. I've arranged to go on a tour, so I'll have a guide. I won't get lost."

"But why do you do these things without consulting me?"

"Note how you're reacting now that I have told you. That's the reason. I avoid unpleasantness as long as possible."

"Won't you tell me where you're going?"

"No, you wouldn't approve of that either. If there's any necessity to phone me, Cary has my itinerary."

"Why don't you make Cary your manager? She seems to be the only one who has your confidence."

Genna laughed again. "Thanks for the suggestion. I may do that. Now run along, Jim. I have to dress for the concert."

The next day Genna deliberately delayed her departure from Frankfurt until she was sure that Jim and the rest of her staff were on their way home. Now she had two hours to wait at the hotel before taking a taxi to the airport. Too fidgety to stay in the room, she checked out and asked the clerk to store her luggage while she shopped.

She wanted to buy Evan a gift, but she had no idea where to find it. She turned right at the hotel's entrance because she thought she'd seen some shops in that direction. Two American servicemen immediately fell in step with her.

"Hi, Miss Ross. We saw your concert last night. It was great," one of them said in a voice marked by a deep southern drawl. His buddy towered over the southerner by at least a foot. She stopped. "Thanks, guys. Now, you just run along and do whatever you intended to do. I don't need an armed escort this morning."

They grinned at her. "Maybe you do," the southerner said, "and we aren't kidding," he added, his face sobering. "Lots of people here resent Americans, and there are always terrorist groups around. You'd wouldn't make a bad hostage, ma'am."

"Well, come on then. Tell me where I can find a gift for that special guy in my life." She made the statement to discourage the soldiers, but it had the ring of truth.

The tall soldier moaned. "Might have known there would be a special guy. There's a jewelry shop close by. It's too expensive for us, but you probably could buy something."

Genna laughed. "I don't care how much it costs, but he probably would."

Once inside the store, the choice wasn't hard to make. She had eyes for only one item. "I'll take the black onyx ring with the diamond in the center." It was a massive ring of white gold, but it wouldn't look too large on Evan's brawny hand.

The soldiers escorted Genna back to the hotel. "Sure nice to run into you, Miss Ross. Hope we can catch one of your concerts when we're back in the States."

She signed two of her cards. "If you ever do, use these as free tickets for you and your family with my compliments, and be sure and let me know you're there."

"You're the greatest, Miss Ross. And a Merry Christmas to you."

Intending to escape her fans for three days, Genna had registered for the tour as Genevieve Wooten. By the time she settled into the first-class section of the jumbo jet, however, Genna wondered if that were possible. During check-in procedures and the hour's wait in the airport, numerous people had approached her asking for autographs and even handouts; many others simply stared at her in perplexity. Fortunately only Genna and an elderly German couple who didn't speak English occupied the compartment so Genna had a peaceful flight.

Genna awakened with a start when the pilot's

message sounded. "Arrival at Tel Aviv in fifteen minutes. Flight attendants, please ready the cabin for landing."

Genna rushed to the restroom and tried to repair her makeup and straighten her hair. Her suit looked as if she'd slept in it as she had! At least she'd have time to shower and change clothes before she saw Evan. The brochure indicated he would be on tour this morning.

Moving slowly with the crowd up the ramp to the passenger area, she heard a shout, "Veevie!"

She waved to him as he pushed through the crowd, his arms cradling an enormous bouquet of red roses. Dropping the bouquet on a chair, he pulled her into his arms and squeezed her until she was breathless. The scent of rose petals swirled around them.

"I was so afraid you wouldn't come," he finally whispered.

"Why? I told you I'd be here."

"Just a worrier, I guess. Anyway, I'm so glad you are. Let's go find your luggage. We don't want to waste a minute of our time together."

"Have you been having a good time?"

"Wonderful," he answered as he guided her through the terminal and down to the luggage area. "We toured Galilee yesterday and took a boat ride on the Sea of Galilee, but it was a calm trip, nothing to remind us of the time Jesus stilled the waters."

"I supposed you'd be on tour this morning; I didn't expect you to be here."

"The others are visiting the ruins of Qumran this morning, but I skipped it."

"Skipped it! Why, Evan, that's where they discovered the Dead Sea Scrolls. That was one of the highlights of the trip."

"Maybe, but having you here is a highlight for me. I had to see you the minute you arrived. Besides, tomorrow we'll be doing sightseeing around Jerusalem. You know, if we return in time, we'll go with the group this afternoon to Masada."

Genna rubbed her face against the sleeve of his coat. "Thanks for being here, Evan. It's nice to be wanted."

"You are."

The tour members greeted Genna warmly, not recognizing her as a singing star, and accepted at face value Evan's explanation that she was a friend.

The tour of Masada took more time then Genna had envisioned, but she felt swept up immediately into the drama of the story. Some of the ruins, the guide explained, dated to 76 B.C., but most of the fortress had been built by Herod the Great. The story of the 960 Jews who had committed mass suicide rather than submit to the Romans stunned Genna, but their courage inspired her to stand firm in her faith against Jim and others who might criticize her.

The evening was free, and after a meal with the others at the hotel, Genna and Evan strolled through the bazaar section of Tel Aviv.

"Help me buy some gifts for Michelle," Evan said. "You should have good ideas."

"I don't know much about children, but I'll help."

They held hands and swung their arms rhythmically. "I feel like a boy myself," Evan admitted. "Do you realize, Genna, that we've never had any fun together?"

"Except tonight. Everybody's supposed to be kids at Christmas. Shall we?" Evan accepted the challenge. They walked from booth to booth buying trinkets for Michelle.

Arriving back at the hotel, they parted in a happy mood. Evan was right; they'd never had any fun before.

The tour guide briefed them at breakfast. "A full day ahead of us, folks. We'll spend the day looking at sites around Jerusalem, and tonight we'll attend services in Bethlehem Square. If any of you wish, we can arrange for a trip to Shepherd's Field about midnight."

"I'd like to go," one woman said, "but how safe is it?"

"As safe as you are anywhere in Israel, I think."

"Evan, let's go," Genna said softly. "It will be wonderful to be on the hillsides around Bethlehem on Christmas Eve. The manmade places are interesting, but I want see the stars and imagine that I can hear the message the angels brought to the shepherds."

He nodded. "That's what I wanted to do when I booked this tour."

The bus labored up the steep road until they came to the Mount of Olives. While Evan took pictures of Jerusalem and the Kidron Valley, Genna tried to recall some of the things that had happened on this site.

In her imagination, she, too, went to sleep while Jesus prayed alone. From this point, Jesus must have mourned over the Jews' failure to accept Him as the Chosen One. She stood with the apostles and watched

Him ascend into heaven with the promise that He'd return again. She strolled beneath eight old olive trees, the remains of a grove destroyed by some unnamed Roman conqueror. Perhaps this very grove of trees had shaded Jesus, she thought solemnly.

Leaving the mount they drove through the Golden Gate, a replacement of one through which Jesus traveled during His triumphant journey into Jerusalem. She held tightly to Evan's hand as they walked along the Via Dolorosa, partly because of the rough street, but mostly because she wanted to share his quiet strength as she contemplated the road that Jesus followed to Calvary.

Would she have been as brave as Simon of Cyrene, who at this point was commanded to carry the cross? Was it here that Jesus told the women of Jerusalem not to weep for Him but for themselves? At the Church of the Holy Sepulchre, she bowed her head wondering if Jesus had really lain there.

Visiting the scenes of His sacrifical suffering seemed to give more emphasis to his birth as they at last entered the old square of Bethlehem to participate in the service at the Church of the Nativity. Genna refused to let the sight of many soldiers guarding the area spoil her worship. God's Son, born as a tiny baby, might not have been pleased with the ostentatious splendor of the church, but on this night of nights, Genna ignored the trappings man had added and envisioned a beautiful peasant woman and her newborn child.

Darkness had completely fallen when they left the church, and a few of the more adventurous tourists followed their guide to the countryside. The stars overspread the sky like a tablecloth. Genna backed up to Evan and he pulled her close for warmth. The few tourists who had braved the danger and the cold to come to Shepherd's Field clustered around a huge bonfire on the land that was reportedly still on the records as belonging to Boaz. Was she standing where Ruth had once gleaned in the field of the man who would become her husband? Although Genna knew that God as Sovereign of all the world was as close to her in Nashville as any place, why then did she feel so much closer to Him here?

Softly, Genna began to sing, "It Came upon the Midnight Clear." One by one the shivering group joined in singing many of the traditional carols, ending with the popular spiritual, "Go Tell it on the Mountain."

Two men presented short sermons. One spoke in Arabic, which was translated by a missionary from the United States, and the other man spoke in English, his message in turn translated by a Christian Arab. A group of native girls passed around cookies and hot chocolate.

As they walked reverently back to the waiting bus, Genna whispered to Evan, "It may have been 2,000 years ago that Jesus came to this place, but tonight He was born for me. I feel my life is now on a new course."

Puzzled, Evan decided to discuss this further with Genna when they reached the hotel. The first floor coffee shop stayed open all night and Evan and Genna sought a quiet corner. After ordering hot tea,

Genna sensed the questions on Evan's lips. "What I meant about having a new course charted for me. . . for the past few months, I've been wondering if I'm using my talents the way I should. I've made lots of money, I have thousands of happy fans, but I'm afraid my music hasn't done anything to glorify God." Pausing to sip her tea, Genna raised her hand to stifle Evan's comments and continued.

"I met Carol Sue, the gospel singer, in Nashville last fall. I attended her concert, and she called me to the stage to sing a duet with her. It was a new experience. Since then, I've occasionally added hymns to my repertoire, and most of my fans have appreciated it." She laughed wryly. "But I'm afraid Jim hasn't."

Evan cleared his throat. "Genna, I don't have any right to ask, but is there anything between you and Jim?"

"Nothing on my part. Jim would like there to be more, but I've told him repeatedly that there never will be. He's a good manager, but the past few months have been stormy between us. I'm not sure I can tolerate him much longer. He's convinced I can't make it without his help, but I think I can. If I should make the transition to gospel music, I'm sure he'll leave me. If I haven't already answered your question, I'm ready for him to resign."

"Is there any hope for us, Genna? Can we truly start over again?"

"It's more complicated than that, Evan. I'm planning to spend this spring in Logan County. I've already told Jim to leave my early summer free. I want to be in the mountains when the redbud decorates the mountainsides, when the dogwood and rhododendron bloom. I'm planning to remodel Grandpap's old house into a vacation retreat. I can't see any reason why we can't forget the past and start over, but it may not happen right away."

Evan lifted her hand and kissed it, his eyes saying more than his lips. "If you're living in Logan County, I'll be parking on your doorstep so much you'll get tired of me."

"I doubt that, but you may get in the way from time to time. Don't worry, if you do, I'll let you know," she said teasingly.

"I'll not interfere, I promise."

"I'm expecting the hills and Miss Amelia to help me decide about my future. I need to meet Michelle, get to know her. She needs to know me. Many things have to be settled before we can make any real plans."

Evan kissed her hand again before he released it and leaned back in his chair sighing deeply. "I know. I've been trying to push my problems out of my mind on this tour, but every night when I'm alone in my room, I start worrying. I'm facing that strike when I return home, and it's apt to become violent. Considering that I might be teetering on financial ruin, we can't make long-range plans anyway."

"That wouldn't matter to me."

"No, but it would to me. A man has to retain his pride, even if he loses everything else. I'd hate to think that the woman I love is a great success in her profession and I fail in mine."

A tremor of distress flitted through Genna's mind. *What would he say if he knew she was the one who'd bailed him out of his former crisis*?

"Evan, let's not spoil our last few hours together by discussing our problems." She reached into her purse. "Here's your Christmas present."

"Sweetheart, this is beautiful," he said as he unwrapped the sparkling ring. He slipped it on the second finger of his left hand. "A bit too small for that finger," he said, "but I can have a jeweler change that at home."

He reached into the pocket of his coat. "I have something for you, too, but I'm afraid it doesn't compare with your gift." Genna's fingers trembled as she opened the blue velvet box to reveal a string of beautifully matched pearls.

"I bought those in Egypt a few days ago."

"You probably don't remember the only other gift you gave me," she said. She reached for the chain around her neck and pulled out the ring he'd given her years ago.

He stared at it. "No, I hadn't forgotten, but I supposed you'd thrown it away years ago."

"I couldn't bring myself to throw away the ring or to forget your promise that someday you'd buy me something better. I had to wait a long time, but that day has come at last."

"I've heard Michelle talk about a new line of Genna Ross jewelry that features opals . . ." he said musingly.

He pulled his chair close to hers. No other guests shared the room with them and even the waiters were out at the moment. As he caressed her lips with his, he whispered, "I'll be waiting impatiently until the dogwood bloom."

nine

The Genna Ross Opal Fire jewelry collection was ready for distribution in mid-March and the company feted Genna at a gala reception in her Nashville hotel. More than a dozen locked cases of the new jewelry were on display in the lavishly decorated ballroom.

The invitation list included all country music stars who made their home in Nashville, as well as jewelry salespeople from around the country. As she stood in the receiving line greeting friends and strangers, Genna looked up with delight when she saw Carol Sue.

"We're still going to have that talk someday," the gospel singer said, "but you're too busy tonight."

"Yes, and I leave tomorrow for another round of concerts."

"Congratulations on your jewelry. I've ordered several sets."

After the well-wishers left, Genna took time to examine the collection. She ordered watches for both Lori and Cary. The goldtone metal case and adjustable bracelet were enhanced by an opal-studded watch face.

Most of the jewelry was designed for women, but she searched for something to send Evan. She finally decided on a masculine cluster ring that combined New Zealand white opals and rubies. The way Jim looked at her when she chose the ring, he obviously thought the gift was for him.

He followed her to the apartment after the reception, and though she was too tired for further conversation, she couldn't wait any longer to discuss her future. Her relations with him had become more and more strained during the winter months, and she dreaded the emotional strain that would necessarily result from their parting. Only one thought propelled her to begin: Three more appearances and she was heading for home and Evan.

"Jim, I think it's only fair to tell you the career change I'm considering. I know you'll disapprove, but you can make your own plans accordingly."

"What have you done now that you haven't told me?"

Genna stifled her anger and answered evenly, "Nothing, but I'm telling you now what I may do. I'm seriously thinking of going into gospel music."

She had expected a verbal onslaught, but hardly the look of horror that crossed his face. Never before had she seen Jim speechless.

"You have to be kidding," he sputtered out finally.

"No, I'm not. This summer will be a decision time for me in many ways. If I'm convinced that this is God's will for my life, in the fall when I start touring again, it will be as a gospel singer."

"You're talking like a fanatic, Genna! What does God have to do with your success? I've made you a great star, and I won't let you throw it away. Think of the rest of us."

"There's no reason you can't continue as you have. I'll need a manager, a secretary, and a band, no matter what I sing."

"You'll lose millions of dollars!"

"I don't care."

"Well, I care. I won't let you do it."

Jim's emphatic statement indicated that the matter was closed, but Genna simply smiled at him.

"I've been wanting to tell you," Jim continued, "I've talked to a publisher who wants to do your life story. They've had a ghost writer following your concerts and checking into your past. They're ready to run the story. All you have to do is sign the contract."

A hot flush of anger flooded Genna's body. "I told you I didn't want a book," she shouted angrily. "How dare you set someone to investigating me! I've seen you at work too long. No book, and that's final. Remember this, Jim. If a publisher runs that book without my permission, I'll sue them and fire you."

The heated exchange only heightened Genna's desire for the mountains, and she thought about home all the next day as they traveled to her next appointment. When they finally checked into their hotel for the night, she sank into a soft chair and closed her eyes. In her mind she climbed to Pinnacle Rock and smelled the warm scent of the earth as the March sun warmed it;a few serviceberry trees were putting forth their white blossoms.

"Oh, Evan," she whispered, "why aren't you a letter writer?" They had contacted each other infrequently during the winter months. She hesitated to telephone him during the day at the office, and her evenings were fairly occupied with her concert tour.

The newspapers had been full of the strike against the Sullivan Mining Company. Pickets had been up for months, and Genna knew this posed a severe drain on Evan's already strained finances. She wanted to send him some money, but she didn't dare interfere again. Once a picture had appeared in a Chicago paper showing Evan crossing the picket line while his workers shouted obscenities at him. He looked as if he'd aged years since Christmas. Since that time he'd been sequestered in the mine buildings.

Finally the desire to talk to him became so strong that she dialed the number of Sullivan Mine No. 2. He answered the phone.

She drew a breath of relief. "Evan, I've been so worried about you. Are you all right?"

"Physically, yes, but not mentally."

"Are you busy now? Do you have time to talk?"

"Nothing but time. I'm a prisoner in my own office. I'm afraid to leave for fear they'll wreck the whole operation."

"Isn't there anyone with you?"

"I have a security force protecting the place. I'm hoping that the strike will soon be over; we have meetings scheduled between management and union representatives almost every day."

"It's almost time for me to come home. I hope you aren't still having trouble then. I want to spend some time with you, Evan."

"And I need you. We'll arrange to be together somehow."

"Is there anything I can do? Maybe I shouldn't

mention it, but I could help you financially. I know this strike must be a drain on your resources."

"No," he said determinedly. "I won't have that between us. We have enough of the past to overcome, Genna. I won't be dependent upon you."

Genna's hands trembled. *What if he found out she'd helped him once? Would that destroy all they'd gained so far?*

"How's Michelle managing in this situation?"

"She's all right. I'm happy you've been writing to her. I want the only two women in my life to like one another."

"I'm looking forward to meeting her."

A thud sounded on the line, accompanied by a scrambling noise, and Genna heard the clatter of the phone as it fell.

"Evan! Evan!" she screamed over and over. The line went dead. She frantically dialed again and received a busy signal.

Cary entered the room. "It's time to dress, Genna." Then she noted Genna's agitation. "What's the matter?"

"I was talking to Evan, there was a shot and the line went dead. He's in that miners' strike, you know. I have to find out what happened to him. Get the travel agency on the line, I'm going to Evan."

"Genna Ross has never run out on a concert before. You'd better think twice."

"But how can I sing when my heart is in shreds?"

"That's where the acting comes in. You've been talking about your renewed faith in God. Now's the time to trust Him. Maybe the telephone line was cut by the shot. When you panic like this, you're listening to the devil instead of to God."

Genna blinked back the tears. She needed Cary's common sense to calm her hysteria.

"You're scheduled to go home in a week, aren't you?"

At Genna's nod, she continued, "Then settle down. After tonight's show, try to telephone and see what has happened."

Genna never knew how she made it through that night's performance. In spite of the praying she did, it was the hardest show of her career. She trembled all over when she finally reached her room at the hotel. She submitted to Cary's ministrations, which usually soothed her tired mind and spirit, but nothing seemed to help.

One thought occurred to her but she quickly dismissed it. It was past eleven o'clock, and Ben and Ivy would long since have gone to bed. There was nothing they could tell her now, and there was nothing she could do but wait until morning. After a sleepless night, Cary greeted her with a breakfast tray and a suggestion.

"Why don't you call the coal mine again? By now the telephone line may have been repaired. Evan may even answer your call."

"Cary, I don't know what I'd do without you. I'm going to miss you this summer."

After trying for two hours without success to reach anyone at the mine, she finally received an answer.

"This is Genna Ross. May I speak to Mr. Sullivan?" she asked, her voice trembling in spite of herself.

"I'm sorry, ma'am. He isn't here."

"Can you tell me where he is? We were talking by phone last night and suddenly the line was dead. I'm concerned about him."

After an uncomfortable hesitation, the man said, "He's in the hospital."

Genna gasped, and her heart pounded until she could scarcely breathe.

"He was shot in the back last night. He's in stable condition, but he will be in the hospital for several days."

After she found out the name of the hospital, Genna thanked the man and hung up. Relieved to know that he was alive, Genna searched out Cary to tell her the news. Cary handed her a newspaper before she got a word out.

"We could have found out about him by reading the paper. Here's an account of the whole thing." Genna grabbed the paper and hurriedly scanned the article.

The reporter concluded, "The only good thing to be gained from the heinous attack on Sullivan seems to be that the tide of public opinion has swung toward the mine management. Even union officials have condemned the wounding of this man who has done so much for the Appalachian coal miners."

Remembering that Angela Keefer was the business administrator at Evan's hospital, Genna put in a call to her.

"Calm down, Genna," Angela's voice reassured. "I don't think he's on the critical list. Hold on a minute while I make some inquiries." Genna drummed her fingers on the table earning her a resigned glance from Cary, but the minutes seemed interminable until Angela spoke again.

"I talked to his doctor, and Evan is in no danger of dying. The bullet has already been removed, and fortunately it missed any vital spot. Go on with your tour, he's in good hands."

Genna wilted with relief. "You're a good friend. Don't tell anyone I telephoned, but I had to know."

Before she left the hotel to travel to her next concert, Genna wired a huge bouquet of flowers to Evan at the hospital. She wanted to talk to him but decided that would have to wait until she could see him. *In less than a week, in less than a week,* the wheels of the bus seemed to say, and they would be together.

At the end of the last scheduled concert, Genna kissed Cary goodbye and shook hands with Jim and Lori and the members of her band. She wondered fleetingly if they would ever be together again. Jim had orders not to make any more appointments for her until she contacted him. She had given her employees a three-month paid vacation; before that time elapsed she would have her decision made. With a light heart Genna headed for the mountains.

"Yes, Mr. Sullivan is still a patient in the hospital," the nurse on duty told her. "Room 135."

Feeling as if she were on wings, Genna swept down the hall. Ever since his hospitalization, she had envisioned herself as his private nurse. The strike had been settled and the miners had agreed to a new contract. That would relieve Evan of his worries, and they could have a few months to find each other again.

She knocked on the closed door and it opened slightly. A youthful face peered at her. "My daddy is asleep. What do you want?"

So he didn't need her after all. This was the other woman in his life.

"Is that you, Michelle? This is Genna Ross. May I come in, please?"

The door swung open and gray eyes so like Evan's peered up at Genna. "Gee, Miss Ross! You're more beautiful than your pictures. Come in."

Genna forgot Michelle when she saw Evan lying on his back in the hospital bed. The intravenous tubes leading down to his arm brought home to her the certainty of his accident.

"Is he all right?" she whispered to Michelle.

"The doctor says so, but he lost lots of blood."

She couldn't stay here any longer without doing something foolish, so Genna backed toward the door. She wanted to throw her arms around him, she wanted to cry, but she couldn't do anything except stare at him. Michelle's presence was a problem. *What had he told her about them*?

"I'll come back when he's awake."

"But he'll want to see you," Michelle cried loudly, and Evan opened his eyes.

A smile lit his face, and he didn't look nearly as ill as Genna had thought at first. He held out his hand to her, and Genna reached for it blindly, blinking back the tears. She was conscious of Michelle's eyes upon them.

"Are you all right, Evan?"

"Doctor says I can go home in a few days. Are you home to stay?"

"Perhaps until the end of summer, or at least long enough to remodel Grandpap's house and make those important decisions I told you about. Our tour schedule has been so heavy that I haven't had time to think."

"You look tired, Genna. Time you had a little rest."

"You have a good nurse, I see," Genna said with a smile in Michelle's direction.

"The best. She says she's going to take care of me after I go home, but I say she's going back to school. We'll see who wins."

Leaving the two of them together, Genna felt a pang of jealousy. Michelle fit into his life as she never could. Already Genna missed the excitement of the tour circuit, and she hadn't been away from it a week. Could she bury herself here in Logan County even for Evan? Would he expect her to give up her career? That was something they hadn't discussed, but it would have to be settled.

When Genna passed the Sullivan No. 2 mine, she noticed many cars near the entrance. Ben and Ivy would know what was happening, Genna thought, as she made her way down their winding dirt road.

"You came at a terrible time," Ben said. "There's goin' to be big trouble at the Sullivan mine, so I hear. I feared you'd be mixed up in hit when you came along the road."

"What do you mean?"

"Best I can hear, the miners are intendin' to wreck hit tonight. I'm glad Sullivan's in the hospital;

leastways, he won't get hurt again."

"But I thought the strike had been settled."

"The miners ain't happy with the contract agreement. They're disregardin' union orders and have walked out on a wildcat strike," Ivy said.

"What are they going to do?"

"I ain't for sure," Ben said.

Genna headed for her car. "I'm going down there."

"No, Veevie, no!" Ivy called, running toward her. "It's no place for a woman."

"Maybe not, but it might be the place for Genna Ross. I have many fans in this county, perhaps they'll listen to me."

She was already guiding the Mercedes out of the yard when Ben jumped in beside her. "If you're goin,' I'll go along. Veevie, why can't you get Sullivan out of your system?"

"He's an old friend."

"Not old enough for you to risk your life to save his property."

They heard sporadic shots before they arrived at the mine. "What's your plan?" Ben shouted at her.

She had the window down, and at the speed she was traveling the noise in the car made it difficult to carry on a conversation.

"I don't have one."

"Just like a woman. We're goin' to get into a mess of trouble."

"No one asked you to come along." When their way was blocked by a barrier of vehicles, Genna hurriedly parked the Mercedes. She heard shouting from the mine buildings and she ran toward the commotion,

Ben at her heels. More than a hundred miners were crowded near the fence surrounding the mine; facing them was a much smaller force of security men.

Evan would have been the target of this confrontation, Genna thought, as she prayed her thanks that he was still in the hospital. She edged her way to the front of the crowd wondering what she could do. Spying a dump truck turned on its side in front of the gate, she whispered to Ben, "Help me up on it."

A miner at the fence held a microphone and she grabbed it from his hand as Ben hoisted her to the truck bed. Although she hadn't sung without music since she was a girl, she swung into her song as readily as if she had the band as a back-up. As she sung a few verses of several hymns, the shouting lessened and the miners left the fence to crowd her improvised stage.

"It's Genna Ross," a young miner shouted.

"That's right," she called back with a smile. "Have a favorite song you'd like to hear?"

"What about 'One-Man Woman?'"

She sung his request, and then another and another until she sensed their anger abating. Finally when she held their attention, and she said, "Men, I grew up in this county in the home of a coal miner, and he taught me that miners didn't want women meddling in their affairs. But I can't stand aside tonight and watch you destroy yourselves and this business. Think how many of you have worked for Sullivan Mining. Consider the people in this county who've had only good from your employers.

"Stick with the bargaining table a little longer,

guys. Evan Sullivan is fair. He'll give you everything he can, but his back is to the wall. Too many mines in this state have closed. If you destroy this one, you'll never have a chance to work here again."

"She's right, men, let's go home and sleep on it."

The crowd dispersed quickly, and a miner helped her off the truck. If it hadn't been for Ben's steadying hand, her shaky legs wouldn't have carried her back to the car. She'd saved Evan's mine for him again, but this time he might find out. She didn't need his thanks, but she did need his pride as a man. There would be no hope for them if that were gone.

ten

Genna walked hesitantly up the hospital steps. *How would Evan react to her?* Any hope that her appearance at the mine two nights ago would escape public notice had died an unmerciful death. Emblazoned across the local newspaper the next morning was the headline, GENNA ROSS SAVES SULLIVAN MINE FROM DESTRUCTION. In smaller type another headline stated, Sullivan Remains Hospitalized. A picture on the front page showed Genna with microphone in hand atop the makeshift stage.

If Evan had been grateful, he could have let her know. She had waited two days to go see him, but finally reasoned he wouldn't know how to contact her by phone.

She took a deep breath and stopped at Room 135. She walked in the open door. A stranger was in the bed that Evan had occupied.

"I'm sorry," she apologized. "I was looking for Evan Sullivan."

"He went home yesterday."

"Oh, I see . . . ."

She walked down the hallway and stopped briefly to gaze out a window at the narrow, crowded streets below. Why hadn't Evan contacted her before he left? She couldn't erase the question from her mind. He could have reached her through the Fishers if he'd tried. She'd give him a few days of convalescence and then she'd telephone him.

In a way Genna was relieved to have their meeting postponed. The rest of the day she spent in Logan talking to contractors and buying supplies for the renovation of Grandpap's home. She had looked the place over with Ben and they had agreed that part of the back porch could easily be converted into a bathroom. Genna eagerly planned the way the old home would look. Before she went home, she applied for a telephone installation.

For a week Genna did little except roam the woods around her cabin. She climbed each day to Pinnacle Rock, and each time was rewarded with a more breathtaking canvas of nature. The dogwood trees bloomed in increasing white profusion, giving a hint of summer to the otherwise sleeping woodland.

At first she was jubilant seeing the places she'd thought about each spring for years, but how different it was from what she'd always envisioned! Since Christmas she'd thought of Evan's presence beside her as she visited the places of her memories. Try as she might, she couldn't recall the pleasures of youth.

What had Evan said? "We'll have to start over again." Perhaps he was right. Her beloved mountains had not brought the healing she needed in her heart.

Another week passed before she finally had a telephone. There was still no word from Evan, and she had waited as long as she could. She wanted to hear from him even if he didn't want to hear from her.

Impulsively, she telephoned his home in Charleston.

The woman who answered the telephone identified herself as the housekeeper, Inez Gilley.

Genna stated her name and said, "I want to inquire about Mr. Sullivan."

"He's doing quite well, thank you."

"Has he been able to leave the house?"

"He's taken a few short trips in the car."

She certainly wasn't getting much information. "Is Mr. Sullivan at home now? I'd like to speak to him if he is."

"Just a minute, please." It seemed like hours before the woman returned. "Mr. Sullivan is resting at the moment. He doesn't want to take any phone calls."

"Oh . . .well, thank you very much. Would you tell him I have a telephone installed at my summer home now?"

"I'll tell him," the woman said and severed the connection.

Where could she go when her heart was breaking? The one person who came to mind was Miss Amelia.

Every time she entered Miss Amelia's living room and sat on the stool beside her chair Genna felt like a child again. Miss Amelia took her hand, and after they sat in silence for several minutes, she asked, "Genna, what makes you so unhappy?"

"I'm not supposed to be unhappy. I'm the great Genna Ross," Genna said bitterly, "and that means nothing because I can't have Evan Sullivan. Am I just being stubborn, Miss Amelia?"

"No, you're following what your heart desires, but you don't have your priorities in the right place. Tell me, Genna, why did you leave your career this spring?"

"To remodel Grandpap's home. To see if Evan has any place in my future. To assess what I'll do with my singing."

"Why?"

"Why what?"

"Why did you find it necessary to evaluate your career?"

Genna hesitated a long time. The mantle clock ticked away the minutes. It was easy enough to say these words to Jim and Evan, but when she said them to Miss Amelia, Genna had the feeling that she was committed. A statement to Miss Amelia was almost as binding as one she'd make to God.

"I think God is calling me to use my voice for some kind of Christian service." And then a sudden thought shook her. "Have you been praying for that?"

Miss Amelia smiled slightly. "Yes, my dear, I have. I've always lived by Jesus' words, 'Seek ye first the kingdom of God and his righteousness; and all these things shall be added unto you.' Once you acknowledge God's leadership in your life, you'll realize your other desires."

"Does that mean Evan?"

"Not necessarily. Evan may not be in God's plan for you, and you'll give him up if that's the case. You'll cease tearing your emotions apart because of Evan."

"But I love him so much," Genna sobbed, and she lowered her head to Miss Amelia's knees. Genna was conscious of a trembling hand on her head, and she looked up into Miss Amelia's face. Tears lined the wrinkled cheeks.

"Oh, Miss Amelia, did you have to make a choice like this too?"

"Yes, Genna," she replied hesitantly. "Before I came to the mountains, I loved this young man very much, but he made it plain that if I married him, I couldn't be a missionary. In other words, it was God's will for my life or him. Believe me, I wrestled with the problem much as you are doing."

"But you let him go?"

"Yes, and once the decision was made, I wasn't sorry. I've never looked back. I've been happy."

"How am I going to know God's will?"

Miss Amelia picked up the Bible. "The answer is here, Genna. I can't tell you. If you seek God's will, you'll find it."

Genna studied the Bible for days, no nearer a decision than she'd ever been. It was hard to get her mind on her meditation when the papers and television were full of news about Evan. The wildcat strike had been settled and the miners were back at work.

When she heard on the radio that Carol Sue and the Hosannas were scheduled for an appearance in Roanoke, Virginia, she decided to pay a visit to Ivy and Ben.

"Want to take a little trip with me?"

Ben rolled his eyes heavenward. "In that high-powered car?"

Genna couldn't decide if Ben were joking about her fast driving or if he really were afraid of the speed.

"I'll promise to keep to the speed limit. I want to

see the Carol Sue concert in Roanoke, and it will be good for you to have a little vacation. We'd be gone only two days."

When they agreed, Genna telephoned for reservations and they left early the next morning. As she shared Ben and Ivy's first view of the Blue Ridge Mountains, Genna forgot her own turmoil over Evan. After they'd settled into a motel, Genna telephoned the hotel where Carol Sue reportedly had registered. She asked for the singer's secretary.

"This is Genna Ross, and I'd like to make contact with Carol Sue. I'm here in town and, if she has time, perhaps I could pick her up after the concert tonight and we could go out for a light meal." Genna gave the number of her motel and asked the woman to telephone Carol Sue's answer.

Within fifteen minutes the phone rang and the secretary said, "You may pick Carol Sue up here at the hotel at ten-thirty tonight."

While Genna watched the concert, she kept trying to put herself in the place of Carol Sue. Could she possibly present a concert that was entertaining yet at the same time spiritually stimulating? Carol Sue had a rare gift that Genna Ross might not have. When they left the auditorium, a peaceful hush seemed to have settled on the huge crowd and talking was at a minimum. Ben echoed Genna's sentiments when he said, "I feel just like I've been to church."

Genna took the Fishers to their motel and returned to the downtown area. Carol Sue waited for her in the lobby.

"It's great of you to take time for me," Genna said.

"I know how tiring a concert can be, and you did a super job tonight."

"But you also know it's necessary to unwind, so I'm pleased you telephoned."

As Genna maneuvered her way into the traffic lane, she explained, "I've wanted to talk with you for months, but it seems our paths didn't cross. I'm spending the summer at my Appalachian home, and when I knew you were this close, I decided to come to see you."

They left the windows down and the cool wind ruffled their hair as Genna drove at moderate speed down Interstate 81. After about ten miles, she exited and pulled into the lot of a small drive-in restaurant.

"Shall we order and stay in the car to eat? We'll have more privacy that way."

"That's fine. If we go inside, there's bound to be someone who would know one of us."

"Yes, but we'd be panicking if no one wanted to talk to us," Genna countered lightly.

After they received their order at the drive-in window, Genna locked the doors and drove to a secluded but well-lighted section of the parking lot.

"Since I saw your concert last year, I can't put out of my mind that I should be doing something similar."

"I've thought the same thing. Genna, you're a natural for gospel music."

"Would you think I was competing with you?"

Carol Sue laughed. "Of course not. I have more invitations than I can possibly fulfill. There's a need for both of us."

"I've been adding a few gospel songs to my concerts, but this overriding feeling keeps occurring that there should be a change in my repertoire. God knows what He wants me to do, but He hasn't revealed it yet, though I feel pressured to make a decision soon."

"If I were you, I'd stop the agitation and just put yourself at God's disposal. When He has a new place for you, He'll reveal it. In the meantime, why not go on as usual?"

"Sounds reasonable," Genna agreed. "I have several fairs scheduled for August and September, and I'm looking forward to those. I know my manager is desperate to arrange my winter's schedule, but I can't give the word."

"Gospel singing has been a great challenge to me, and you probably would like the change, but don't do anything until you know that it's right for you. I feel in my heart that God has some great plan for your life, and when the opportunity comes, you'll know what it is."

Genna left Carol Sue at the hotel with a lighter heart, and the next morning the feeling of peace was still with her. Taking their time, Genna and Ivy and Ben spent the day driving along the Blue Ridge Parkway. At almost every turnout where they stopped to view the Shenandoah Valley, Ben scratched his head and muttered, "It's a big old world when you see hit from here, ain't hit?"

Genna laughingly agreed it was, but wondered what Ben would think of the world if he'd ever seen it from an airplane. Genna didn't head toward Logan County until it became too dark to see, and they arrived on Mill Creek at a late hour.

"Way past my bedtime," Ben said as he crawled out of the car, "but I had a good time, girl."

A few weeks later, when Genna was returning from Logan where she'd gone to order some supplies, she saw Evan's truck at the mine. She went on by for a mile, then turned and drove slowly back. All she could do was try. She had to see him at least once more before she put him out of her life.

Just as she pulled in the parking lot she spied Evan a few feet away walking toward his truck. He wouldn't have a chance to avoid her now.

"I'm glad to see you're back at work, Evan. Are you feeling all right now?"

"Yes, thanks," he answered gruffly without looking at her.

Her eyes smarted and she blinked rapidly but she held back her tears. The years in drama school paid off as she said without a tremor in her voice, "Seems to me when we parted at Christmas, I heard something about us starting over again. Have you changed your mind about that, Evan?"

"This is no place to talk," he muttered, still not meeting her gaze.

"You don't seem to want to talk elsewhere, but I'll be at home this evening."

"I'll be there at seven o'clock."

Three hours until seven o'clock, but she supposed she could survive. She spent the hours praying, and by the time Evan arrived, she had chosen her words carefully. She knew now that she had to sing, and if

Evan couldn't accept her and her successful career, she'd have to give him up. God had given her the talent to sing and she couldn't shove it aside, not even for Evan. When he drove into the yard, she whispered, "All right, Lord. Not my will, but yours be done."

She took Evan on a tour of the house, which didn't take long, and they seated themselves on the porch. The June night was aburst with lightning bugs, singing insects, and the fresh smell of the yellow rambler rose at the end of the porch.

When the silence lengthened between them, Genna said at last, "I think I have the right to know why you've changed toward me."

He turned angrily toward her. "As if you didn't know! How do you think I feel to be obligated to the woman I love? Genna, why did you go to the mine that night?"

"If I hadn't gone, you wouldn't have a mine left."

"I'll admit the truth of that, but that doesn't make it any easier to take."

"Would you have preferred to have your operations wrecked? To have no place for the miners to go now that the strike is over? What's bothering you, your pride? I have reason to remember that your pride has always stood in your way; you were always concerned what people thought about the Sullivans."

The words were bitter in her mouth. *Would she never forget Evan's rejection of her on Pinnacle Rock?*

Evan continued as if he hadn't heard her. "And then to find out that you were the one who'd given me the money to save the mining operations! I thought the accountant had secured a loan until I asked him the other day about paying it back. When I found out he didn't even know where the money had come from, I stormed into Blankenship's office and demanded the truth. Genna, why did you meddle in my business?"

A lump rose in Genna's throat, but she swallowed convulsively and said, "Let me ask you again. Would you have preferred to lose your business rather than to accept help from me?"

He turned away, and Genna continued. "'Pride goeth before destruction, and an haughty spirit before a fall.' Maybe this isn't the time to remind you of that, Evan, but you're being foolish. I had the name and the voice to convince those miners to avert a problem that would have ruined you and them. I had the money to save you when I wouldn't let you strip my property. I felt responsible for that problem because of the promise I'd made Grandpap. Was the only reason you liked Veevie Wooten because she had nothing? Yes, Evan, Veevie Wooten would be completely dependent on you. But I'm not Veevie Wooten anymore, not the crooked-toothed, ill-spoken, plain girl of the past. I'm Genna Ross now, and nothing can change that. I came back this spring hoping to revive the past. The first thing I learned is that one can't erase twelve years."

"I know," he said. "I wish I could."

"I thought we could when I came home. But this month I've wrestled with my problems, and I've reached an answer. I won't let you hurt me again. If you want to accept me as I am, money and career, then we might be able to begin again. If you expect me to be Veevie Wooten, I'm sorry but I'm not giving up everything I've gained for you. I'm ready to forget that we once meant something to each other."

"Do you really mean that?" he asked, surprise in his voice.

"I really mean that. If you need to think about it, all right, but I don't intend to waste any more time grieving over what we lost. I'm going to make a new start, with or without you."

He reached for her and pulled her into his arms. "Then make it with me, Genna. I don't want to lose you again. Forgive me for being angry."

Genna stifled the tears welling up from her heart. *She couldn't give in yet.* "But how do you feel about my career? One of the things I've had to deal with this month is what direction my work will take. God wants me to continue singing, not in the same way, perhaps, but for His glory. How will you feel about that? Will you accept that my life won't always be subject to what you want?"

"I'll admit that won't be easy. I want to marry you, Genna, I want you in my life always. I won't like it if you're gone for weeks at a time. I'd want us to be together, but if you'll marry me, I'll accept you as you are."

She kissed him lightly on the cheek. "I won't want to be away from you either, but it may come to that. God hasn't revealed what He wants me to do, but I'm expecting an answer soon. I had to acknowledge that He came first in my life, even before you, Evan, as much as I love you."

"But you will marry me?"

"Let's give ourselves a month. That's when I have to notify my band about my plans. We can see each other as often as possible, and I can spend some time with Michelle too. I guess I want to see how I like having to share you with someone else. I need to know that from the outset."

Evan smiled and drew her close again, his hand caressing the waves of her hair. As she returned Evan's embrace, Genna realized, perhaps for the first time, that she embraced her future as well.

eleven

Genna held the letter from Cary for five minutes before she opened it. She corresponded regularly with Cary, but none of the other letters had filled her with such dread.

A newspaper clipping fell out into her lap when she opened the envelope. The headlines of the article said it all: GENNA ROSS LIFE STORY TO BE PUBLISHED BY GARNER PRESS. Before she read the article, with trembling fingers she scanned Cary's note. "I doubt you've been reading many newspapers this summer and perhaps you missed this. Did you know anything about it?"

According to the article, the book had been written by Joe Bagley, a ghost writer, who did biographies of many famous people for Garner. Genna assessed the situation trying not to lose her temper. She mustn't act rashly. Maybe the publisher was putting out an unauthorized biography, but Garner was a reputable publisher. She doubted they'd act in an unethical manner.

She quickly contacted George Blankenship by telephone.

After he heard her story, he asked, "What exactly do you want me to do?"

"I'd like for you to call the publisher, as my attorney, and inquire where they received the permission to do my life's story. When I have that information,

I'll decide what to do next."

Blankenship obtained the information quickly and got back to her within an hour. "Your manager, Jim Slater, signed the contract authorizing the book."

"But I told him not to do it. I don't want the book."

"How much authority have you given him as your manager?"

"I'd have to check the contract, but I feel sure I gave him only authorization to book my personal appearances and schedule recordings."

"Perhaps the best thing to do is to let the book be published. If you make too big a fuss, they'll probably publish anyway. Even if you sue them, all the publicity will make people more determined to read the book."

"You may be right, but I don't think a company like Garner would want to be on my blacklist. Will you write a letter to them, saying that I had not authorized the publication, and that my manager knew I didn't want a book?"

Now that her relations with Evan were mending, she didn't want anything to smear their youthful romance. She'd read too many biographies, written to be made into movies or to make money for recording companies, where the truth was stretched to make a sensational story. Even if the book related accurately her romance with Evan, he wouldn't like it.

Blankenship heard from Garner Press within a week, and he contacted her by phone.

"They said they were very sorry that Miss Ross was displeased about the book. They had been led to believe that you were agreeable to the publication.

They will halt printing until your personal approval is given, but they asked if you'd be kind enough to read the proofs to see what you find objectionable."

"Yes, I'll read the proofs," Genna told Blankenship. "If they'll agree to my edited copy, I'll let them go ahead; otherwise, I'll take other legal action. May I have an appointment to see you tomorrow? I have some other work that can't wait any longer."

Within a week she had to notify her staff about contracts, and she'd made her decision. Jim and Lori had to go, and since she didn't know what type of singing she'd be doing, she had decided to terminate the contracts of the band too. If she sang only folk songs and gospel music, she could do very well with a pianist. She would keep Cary on the payroll for at least a year.

The next day when Blankenship read copies of the contracts, which had been forwarded from her accountant in Nashville, he assured Genna that her intentions were legal. Just as she thought, the contracts could be terminated with a month's notice and two months' pay.

"Since I want to be fair, pay them three months' salary. My accountant will take care of the details, but I'd like you to write the letters."

The proofs of her biography came in the mail the next week, and Genna spent two days going over them. Obviously, the author had visited the area, and the book would contain photographs of her birthplace, the schools she'd attended, and even the little Bethel Church. Several of her childhood acquaintances had been interviewed, including Angela Keefer, but not a word was mentioned about Evan. They'd kept their secret well, and she breathed a sigh of relief.

Actually the book didn't say much about her girlhood years. The author had picked up her story when she started to drama school in California and followed carefully her rise to fame. The manuscript was well written and factual with only a few exceptions, and within a few days she sent the proofs back to the publisher with her corrections and approval.

As soon as Blankenship mailed the letters to her staff, Genna telephoned Cary.

"I wanted you to know in advance about it, Cary."

"But why are you keeping me? What are we going to do?"

Genna laughed. "I don't know. God hasn't told me that yet, but you'll draw your salary until I know. Whatever I do, I want you with me."

Genna had expected Jim to telephone, not to appear at her door. When he stepped up on the porch one afternoon in late July and knocked on her screen door, for a moment she was relieved the door was locked.

At a loss for words, at last she said, "Come in, Jim." *Perhaps she owed him something*, she thought.

He surveyed the room. "So this is where you've been wasting your time. Quite a step down for Genna Ross, isn't it?"

His comment gave Genna time to control her emotions, and she laughed. "You should have seen the house before I remodeled it. That's been one of my projects this summer."

"Genna, you can't do this to me," he said as he sank heavily into Grandpap's old rocker.

"But I have done it," she replied. "You can't say I hadn't warned you. I'd hesitated to fire you, but when you went ahead with that book contract without my consent, that was the last straw."

"That was too great an opportunity to lose. Garner Press does biographies of only top stars."

"I had already told you I didn't want any book, Jim. When I told the editor that you had no right to sign that contract, he agreed they wouldn't publish the biography. However, I've read the proofs and didn't find them objectionable, so I've given my consent."

"That didn't do my rating with Garner any good."

"You should have thought of that before you double-crossed me."

"Are you still planning on becoming the next Carol Sue?" Jim could not contain his old teasing nature, despite the tone of the visit.

"I don't think so, but I'll be going into some kind of Christian singing."

"Have you hired another manager yet?"

Genna shook her head. A strong breeze swept down the hollow and rattled the windows of the cabin. A cardinal's clear call sounded from the maple tree in the front yard, while a woodpecker drummed on a distant dead bough. She tried to detach herself from the room. Change had always been hard for her, and Jim had been part of her life for five years.

"Then why can't I continue as I always have? I'll not disregard your wishes again."

"It's too late, Jim. You were a good manager until

you let your personal feelings get in the way. You're either critical or jealous of every move I make, and I'm tired of it. I'm sorry, because we did make a good team once, but no more."

"If you'd have married me, we would have made a better team."

Genna shook her head. She had been expecting Evan, and she heard his footsteps on the porch. He'd been away for two weeks and had no idea about her biography. When he entered the room, she couldn't help comparing him to Jim. Evan represented the security she had always needed. Jim would always remind her of those exciting days of reaching stardom, but also of the misery and bitterness of the years when Evan was only a memory.

"Jim, if you remember, you met Evan Sullivan in Columbus last winter. Evan and I haven't made final plans, but we're sort of engaged to be engaged." She walked to Evan, and he drew her close in the circle of his arm. "I don't know whether this will make you feel better or worse, but I've loved him since I was sixteen years old, and I'll never stop loving him."

Jim scrutinized them closely. He swallowed hard, and finally said, "I hope you'll be happy." He left the room without another word. Secure in the warmth of Evan's embrace, for the first time, she felt sorry for Jim.

Early the next morning, Blankenship telephoned. "There's a man here who wants to talk business with you, Genna. Is it all right if I send him out?"

"Let me come to your office. When discussing business, I'd prefer to have an attorney present. Is this business anything I'll be interested in?"

"I rather think so." Blankenship sounded excited, and Genna agreed to be at his office within the hour.

The large, florid man in Blankenship's office introduced himself as Lowell Graham. "Miss Ross, we're looking for a place to build a year-round resort in West Virginia, and we think that mountainous area near your home would be ideal. What we have in mind is to build a place that we can tie to the name of a well-known person similar to Dollywood in Tennessee. If you'd allow us to name the resort for you, and you'd make frequent appearances at the hotel, we'd have a winner. The natural area is great for this. We'd appeal to the skiers in winter but plan other activities throughout the year. What do you say?"

"If I'd allow my name on the resort, I'd want some control over it. Are you selling stock in this venture?"

Graham smiled. "We do hope for some local monetary investment. We'd welcome Genna Ross as a stockholder."

"You should know that I am thinking of changing my musical repertoire from country music to gospel."

"Surely you would consider singing the folk songs you've included in the past."

"Yes, at times, but my primary thrust will be gospel music. I'll be touring some, so I couldn't be at the resort every day."

"We're intending to make so much money that you'll want to stay here all the time," Graham said with a smile.

"Logan County could use a boost to its economy now, and what's good for the resort will be good for our area."

"We'll give you several names to choose from, but we're favoring Gennaland."

"I'm going to be on concert tour for the next two months, but I'll notify you of my decision."

Genna broke the news to Evan as soon as he came to see her that night. "What do you think of the idea?"

The eagerness in his eyes warmed Genna's heart. "I know I shouldn't be selfish, and I'm trying to let you decide your own career without any influence from me, but it would make me happy to know you'd be working nearby instead of traveling so many months out of the year."

"Funny how we have the same idea! Yet one thing bothers me—do you believe a resort will ever be successful here?"

"With the Genna Ross name on it, I feel sure it will. That's the reason the promoters want a large name. They like this area, and then to find that you live here cinched the proposition for them."

"Will they be able to find enough land?"

He smiled. "I had a visit from the agent too. They want to buy the property I'm stripping up here on the mountain. It will be a good way to reclaim the area when I've finished. They plan to put a ski lodge on the eastern slope of the mountain; this side wouldn't be changed at all."

"What else do they plan beside the lodge?"

"They want to develop a golf course if they can locate enough level land and to build a tramway across Mill Creek Valley. They're either leasing or buying some of the old Miller property. And, of course, they'll have swimming facilities, tennis, and other recreation at the lodge."

"Good! They'll be doing what I want done, preserving the mountain beauty that I cherish. You know, Evan, if we're married, we can't very well live in this cabin."

"How long before you have to give them an answer?"

"I've put them off until after I've finished my fall concerts. In the meantime, Blankenship is looking into the financial condition of this company."

"What does he think about the resort?"

"He's as excited as he ever gets about anything. He believes it will be a boost to the county's economy."

"It will surely boost my economy. They've offered a lot more for that land than I paid for it. With my finances on a solid footing again, at least that won't stand in our way of happiness."

She kissed him tenderly. "Evan, I'm beginning to believe nothing can stand in the way of our happiness now."

Now that Genna had terminated the contracts with her band, she had a short time to arrange for musical accompaniment for her upcoming state fair concerts. With Lori gone, she would also need a secretary.

Lunching with Angela one day, Genna said, "Here's where I miss Jim. I need a pianist part-time and a secretary part-time, and I haven't had to worry about hiring before. Jim did that. I really don't know where to turn."

"Do you want two different people, or would you

be happy if one person could fill both needs?"

"I'll have to settle for what I can find, I suppose, but I'd like to find one person who's a trained musician and also has business experience. Do you know where I could find such a person?"

The amused expression in Angela's eyes baffled Genna for a moment, and then she shouted, "Would you?"

The other diners in the restaurant looked at Genna, and she flushed and lowered her voice. "I would love to have you, but I wouldn't have considered asking you to give up your job."

"I have a good income from my husband's insurance, and I'd enjoy leaving Woodville occasionally. I haven't traveled much, and I think it would be fun to do concerts with you. Don't worry that it will inconvenience me. I'd love playing while you sing, and I'm sure I could handle your scheduling and other business."

"It sounds like a great idea, but let's not decide until we've practiced together. Shall we try out some music tonight?"

After a few practices, Angela could follow every tempo and inflection of voice that Genna introduced. After renting office space in Logan, Genna set Angela to work in her dual role as secretary.

The first of August they joined Cary in Nashville, and the three women spent the next two months traveling by plane and rental cars to the fairs. Finding this way of travel most satisfactory, Genna placed the big bus on the market.

By the time the tour ended, Genna had made her

decision, convinced that God had made plain His will for her life. She would spend most of her time singing at the resort, booking only occasional appearances away from home. She telephoned her decision to Lowell Graham, and he told her that he'd start immediately proceedings for building the resort.

She wrote Evan a letter, telling him of her plans and her love for him. Tears flowed freely when she wrote the last paragraph. "The past is behind me now, Evan. We've waited a long time and I'm ready to marry you. I love you."

twelve

Soon after Genna returned from her fair concerts the weather turned unseasonably cold. With two nights of frost the turning of the leaves from green to autumn hues was evident. Ben stopped Genna one day when she was returning from her office in Logan.

"I'm goin' to cut a bee tree tonight. Want to come along?"

"Well, Evan is coming to see me this evening. Will it be all right for him to go too?"

"Sure thing. Ivy's goin', so we'll make a party of it."

"It may turn into quite a party if those bees are still active. Aren't you rushing it a bit?"

"After these two big frosts, they won't sting."

"Uh-huh," Genna said unconvincingly. Bee stings or not, she didn't want to miss this nostalgic adventure. One of her earliest memories was tagging along with Grandpap when he climbed the mountains to cut a tree where the wild bees had stored a supply of honey. The hoard from two or three of these trees had kept honey on their table throughout the winter.

Genna telephoned Evan as soon as she arrived at the cabin.

"Sounds like fun," he agreed. "There's supposed to be a full moon tonight . . . ."

"It won't be a romantic walk, I warn you. From my experience, the tree will probably be on the steepest side of the mountain, and our only interest will be in keeping the bees from stinging us."

Evan laughed. "Nonetheless, I'm game. I like anything if I'm in your company. Love you."

"Me, too. See you soon after dark."

Bundled into heavy coats and gloves as protection against the sharp cold, they walked to meet Ivy and Ben at their house. As they started up the mountain trail, Evan asked Ben, "Why do you go at night, and why does it have to be a cold one at that?" He pulled the coat collar around his neck.

"If it's not chilly, the bees will sting you. They're sluggish when it's cold. You cut at night because the weather is colder then."

"I always thought it was to keep the bees from seeing you," Genna said.

"They don't need to see to find you," Ivy commented.

They walked single file in silence, the only sound the rhythmic crunch of their feet on the frosty turf. Genna and Evan carried flashlights, but they were hardly needed. Evan's predicted full moon peered over the mountain and bathed the area in a subdued light.

Ben had his hands full with a crosscut saw and an axe and Ivy carried two buckets. Since only Ben knew the location of the tree, they followed him through the woods. Their destination was a steep point, and when they paused to catch their breath, Ben pointed out some landmarks.

"There's your house, Genna, and ours is right here below us. That's Sullivan No. 2 to the left." Genna had left her porch light on so it was easy to find her house and of course many lights surrounded the coal mine.

Shining his flashlight on the side of a huge tree, Ben said, "See the hole next to that lower limb. That's where the bees go in and out." The tree, which Ben said was a black oak, was about fifty feet tall and the first limb was twenty feet above the ground.

"Ever use a crosscut saw?" Ben said to Evan.

"No, they didn't teach that in engineering school."

"You'll not learn any younger. Be a good experience for you." Ben circled the tree. "First, we have to decide where we want hit to fall. Stuck up on this point like hit is, hit's bound to go downhill whatever we do. Stand back now."

Ben picked up the axe and began to chop the tree trunk about three feet above the ground. When he'd made a sizable gash in the bark, he picked up the saw and said to the two women, "Stand a fur piece off for the tree might buckle and fall backwards. Be ready to run if hit does.

"You take one end of this saw," Ben instructed Evan, "and we'll pull hit back and forth steadylike. When you hear the tree creak a little, help me pull the saw out, then run out of the way. I'll push the tree over if hit's still standin,' but chances are the weight will pull hit down even if hit ain't sawed all the way through."

With a smile in Genna's direction, Evan did as he was told. The tree was about ten feet in circumference, and from Genna's observation, she thought Evan was doing a fine job. Unimpressed, Ben ordered, "Here now! Quit jerkin' on that saw. Do you want to break the teeth outen hit? Pull steady." Evan followed his instructions, and Ben gruffly added, "That's better."

"Come down here, Ivy," Ben called, "and hold the light. I want to see how much farther to saw." Ivy scurried toward the tree and flashed a beam on the trunk and Ben decided he had a few more inches.

The only sound in the forest was the rhythmic hum of the saw as it bit farther and farther into the tree trunk, scattering sawdust at the feet of the two men. Genna saw the top of the tree jerk, followed by a sharp snapping sound.

"Quick, pull out the saw and run!"

Ben was close behind Evan when he reached the women. The old tree hovered between the heavens and the earth for a few moments as though reluctant to give up its commanding position in the forest. At last the pull of its enormous weight was too strong to be withstood, and with a final shudder, it left the spot it had occupied for centuries, crushing the underbrush and smaller trees in its path. The noise of the crash was deafening, but after the tree settled to its final resting place, a strange hush settled over the forest.

Genna broke the quietness by saying softly, "There's something a little sad about it, isn't there?"

"I know," Ivy agreed. "I feel bad every time one of these trees is cut, especially when you realize how many years it's been standin.' "

Ben, practical as always, said, "This is nature's

way. That tree had outlived hits usefulness. Hit was dyin,' or the bees couldn't have found a place in hit. God planned nature this way. The dyin' tree made a home for the bees, and the bees provided food for man. Veevie, I'm expectin' you to help me take the honey."

The tree had been so tall that its uppermost branches had landed on the other side of a small gully forming a bridge from one side to the other. A low, humming sound came from inside the tree, and Ben whistled. "Boy, listen to that buzz. The fall stirred 'em up. Ivy, fill up the smoker and light hit. We're goin' to need hit."

"Explain to me what's going on," Evan said.

Ben pointed to an item shaped like a coffee pot with a set of bellows on one side that Ivy had pulled from a bucket. She stuffed the top of the pot with rags and ignited them with a match.

"That's a smoker," Ben explained. "We'll use it to blow smoke in that hole. As soon as the smoke dulls the bees, I'll cut the trunk of the tree where they have their hoard, and we'll lift out the honey."

Ben took another apparatus from the bucket and pulled it over his head. Genna laughed when she recognized it as the same kind of garb Grandpap had worn: nothing but an old straw hat with some cheese cloth draped over it. Ben tied it around his waist with some heavy string and pulled gloves on his hands.

"There's another one," he said to Genna. "Put hit on. You can hold the bucket."

"Just like I used to do for Grandpap," Genna said excitedly.

Ben found a foothold under the tree and puffed smoke into the hole. The bees hummed angrily, but the noise soon ceased. Using the axe, he cut a slab off the trunk and straddled the tree near the cut he'd made. He motioned for Genna, and she moved to his side carrying a bucket.

Three layers of comb had been made, and Genna saw the bees working sluggishly in and out of the waxy openings filled with amber honey. Using a butcher knife, Ben soon filled one bucket with honey and Genna handed it to Evan who brought the other bucket. When it was filled, Ben laid the slab back over the opening.

"I'm leavin' a third of the honey to keep the bees alive through the winter."

"Will they make honey in this tree again?" Evan asked as they gathered up the buckets of honey and the equipment to head for home.

"Not likely," Ben answered. "Come spring, they'll move on to another tree."

Genna felt the frigid air seeping through her heavy coat. Her breath rose before her face and her hands felt numb. When they reached the Fishers' house, Ivy said, "Let me put some of this honey in a dish and you can take hit home with you."

The cold air urged them along, and Evan and Genna made record time to her cabin. Though it was almost midnight, Genna said, "If you're not afraid to try some of my cooking, come on in, and I'll make some biscuits to go along with our honey. That climb made me hungry."

Evan entered the house and helped her remove her

coat. "Sounds fine to me, but I'm surprised you can cook."

With a saucy look over her shoulder as she entered the lean-to kitchen, she said, "I'll admit I haven't done much, but Grandpap taught me to make biscuits a long time ago. Ivy has been a good teacher this summer."

"Want me to make some coffee?"

"Yes, the automatic brewer is there on the shelf, and the coffee is in the fridge."

The biscuits and coffee were ready in a half-hour and they soon consumed a large portion of the honey Ivy had given them. When they finished, Evan said, "When we're married, Genna, every night will be like this night . . .good companionship and the thrill of being together. I'm ready whenever you are."

"I'm ready too. Let's set the date for early spring."

"Do you think hit will ever stop rainin'?" Ben asked as he sloshed through the water that had collected in Genna's front yard.

Genna met him on the porch, glancing anxiously toward the muddy water roiling down Mill Creek. "The weather report warned of flash floods."

"There ain't no let-up in sight near as I can tell," Ben grumbled as he warmed himself in front of her small fire. "You sure are cozy here. I bet Grandpap wouldn't know the place if he'd come back. Hit helps to have money, don't hit?"

Genna smiled at him. "Yes, it does. I've lived in both extremes, never having enough money, and then having more than I needed. I've leveled off this year.

The royalties from my recordings have rolled in steadily, so I've done very well for having worked only part-time since March."

"Hit's sure good you're goin' to stay here, girl. We like havin' you around, and you'll get all the singin' you want at that resort, time hit opens up."

"They plan to have it finished by next fall. I have agreed to make some personal appearances this winter and next spring, too, but I won't be gone much."

"How about you and Evan? Anything goin' to happen there?"

Genna nodded happily. "Next spring. We want to give Michelle time to get used to the idea, and Evan needs to feel he's on his feet financially. He's too proud to live on my income."

Ben nodded sagely. "Sure, don't blame him. A man likes to provide for his own. So hit looks like things are coming up roses for you."

"I'm almost thirty years old, Ben, so I'm a little late trying matrimony. I hope I can stay hitched, as Grandpap used to say."

Rising slowly from his chair, Ben said, "Better late than never."

"Don't go yet."

"Yeah, got to. I'm goin' to take a look at that dam at the head of the holler. I keep my eye on hit whenever we have lots of rain. I'm afeared of hit."

"Wait until I put on a coat and I'll go with you. I've been in too long today, I've got cabin fever."

Ben's truck churned through the mud as he guided the vehicle up the hollow and the side of the mountain to the sludge dam.

The water was already within an inch of the top. "What if it runs over the fill?" Genna asked, panic in her voice.

."Tain't runnin' over that worries me. I'm afeared the whole thing is goin' to bust one of these days, just like that one at Buffalo Creek several years ago. If hit does, there won't be nothin' left of Mill Creek, 'cept a memory. I wish I'd raised more ruckus about it, but hit's easier to let things go sometimes. I don't worry about hit until hit starts rainin.' "

"It's not your place more than any other person's. But I had no idea this lake got so full when it rains. I've only been up here in the summertime and usually the water level is low then."

Ben was unusually quiet all the way back to her cabin. "Why don't you come and bunk with us tonight, Veevie? You're awful close to that creek, and here on the level, you could get some high water."

She laughed at his fears. "You sound just like Grandpap. He was always predicting we'd get washed out of this hollow sometime and we haven't yet."

"John Wooten was a right smart man, Genna. He had a good head on him. Better come home with me."

Genna laughed away his fears, but she couldn't clear her mind of worry. She kept the television on to see the occasional flood warnings, and she paced nervously as the rain continued pounding on the roof. She walked out on the porch several times and strained her eyes to see the water. With an occasional flash of lightning to aid her vision, it did seem as if the water were closer to the road each time she looked.

Suddenly the night was shattered by a blast as loud as a dynamite charge. The sound had come from the hollow, and Genna knew her fears had been realized. *The dam had collapsed.*

Gratefully she saw headlights coming up the road, and she laughed nervously. "Good old Ben. Coming to check on me again. I'm getting out of here."

Rapid steps crossed the porch and the door was shoved open. "It's me, Genna," Evan said. "We've got to get out of here. I was coming to check on you, and I heard that blast. I'm afraid the dam has burst."

Genna grabbed his arm. "Listen," she whispered.

After the first blast, quietness had settled around the homestead, broken only by the heavy rain pelting on the galvanized roof. Then they heard a sound resembling the roar of a train coming down the hollow. Evan raced out on the porch and she followed him.

For a moment, Evan was stunned. "Look at that wall of water!" Genna strained her eyes and the lightning flashes illuminated a wall of water about eight feet high mixed with rocks and other debris rolling toward them. Trees snapped like matchsticks as the deluge of water continued unhindered. The destructive wall weaved back and forth from one side of the hollow to the other. When it changed course and headed toward the house, Evan grabbed her arm. "Let's head for the mountain. Even now, we may not make it."

The wall of water hit the front porch and shook the house as soon as they left. Water tugged at Genna's feet, and she slipped backward, but Evan pulled her with him until they reached the cemetery knoll.

"Higher," he gasped. "Nothing can stop that water."

Genna never knew how they were able to climb the mountain, she only knew they had never stopped. Whenever she stopped for breath, Evan would beg, "Hurry, sweetheart."

The batteries in Evan's flashlight were weak and the light flickered often. It was better than nothing, but most of the time Genna stumbled along the darkened trail. Once when she started to slip, she grabbed at a tree for support and the swinging branch struck her sharply in the throat. She cried out but Evan was ahead of her and didn't hear.

The path they followed seemed familiar, and she realized Evan was on the Pinnacle Rock trail. Rain poured over her head, drenching her clothes. When they came to a rock overhang about halfway up the mountain, Evan stopped. "Let's stop here and rest. We'll have some protection from the rain."

He flashed his light around the rocky ledge to be sure that it was free of animals, then he sat down, his back against the wall, and pulled Genna into his arms.

"I'm afraid to imagine what happened to the rest of the valley," Genna said, shivering.

Evan drew her closer and wrapped his jacket around both of them. "Nothing could survive that onslaught of water. Anyone or anything in its path would be destroyed."

A sudden thought occurred to her. "The mine, too."

He laughed wryly. "Yes, this will finish me. I don't know whether to be happy or sad as much trouble as I've had at the mine the last few years. I'm wiped out."

"You still have your strip mining."

"No, I sold that land to the resort company today. That's what I was coming to tell you."

"Then at least we'll have that to look forward to."

"But most important, we'll have each other. If I hadn't arrived when I did, I might have lost you too. That's a loss I couldn't handle, Genna."

"I love you, Evan," she whispered.

"What's the matter with your voice? You don't sound like yourself."

"A tree limb hit me in the throat and I've felt numb ever since. It's an effort to talk."

"We'll stop talking then. Try to rest if you can."

The rain had lessened somewhat by daylight. Genna was drowsy and Evan shook her gently awake.

"Do you feel like walking on to the pinnacle? I'd like to see the damage."

Genna opened her mouth to speak but no words came out. Evan looked at her in consternation. She tried again, but no words, only a squeak.

"Sweetheart," he said, "can't you talk yet?"

She shook her head.

"We'll have to get you to a doctor."

She framed the words with her lips. "How? We'd better see what the valley looks like."

Silently, Evan took her hand and helped her up the mountain trail. Standing beside Pinnacle Rock,

Genna gasped in disbelief. The valley was devastated. They couldn't see an undamaged building and the winding road and the bridges that had crossed Mill Creek were gone. The old mining structure at the base of the mountain had been swept away in the deluge; even the lake where they'd picnicked last summer was empty. The water and heavy debris had roared down the valley leaving behind only a heavy layer of mud.

Mill Creek was overflowing its banks. Genna strained her eyes to see Grandpap's cabin, but she couldn't tell if anything remained. The tipple and the buildings of Sullivan Mine No. 2 had collapsed under the onslaught of the wall of water and debris. For a half-mile on each side of the river, trees and underbrush had been swept away.

"I can't believe this," Genna whispered.

"It's bad enough what's happened to the property, but what about the people? What about the people?"

"Is there any way we can get to Ben's?"

"We can go around the mountain. Are you up to walking?"

Genna merely nodded.

By noon they came out on the point where Ben's trailer had been. Genna felt faint. Half a dozen large trees had been deposited at the site. She turned away with a sick heart, and Evan's arm comforted her.

She roused herself when she heard a shout.

"Look!" Evan said. "There's Ben up there, waving to us."

Genna started running toward the spot, but Ben called, "Stay there, we're comin' down."

"Thank God," Genna whispered. "At least they escaped."

Ben lumbered into the clearing, Ivy at his heels. He grabbed their hands. "I was never so glad to see anyone in my life. I felt sure the water had got you." He turned to Evan. "What'd you make of that? Ever see anything to beat that water?"

Evan shook his head. "Never. Of course the dam must have burst, but I couldn't believe how fast that water traveled."

"Why, hit was more than six feet high, just pushin' everything in front of hit. If hit had to happen, I wish hit'd been in the daylight, so we could have seen."

Ivy reached them by now, and Genna hugged her. "Oh, I'm glad I still have you. Everything else is gone."

"What's wrong with your voice?"

Genna shook her head, and Evan answered, "While we were climbing the mountain last night in the dark, a tree branch struck her in the throat. She hasn't been able to talk well since. It seems as if her throat is paralyzed."

"What'll that do to your singin'?" Ivy asked.

Genna turned startled eyes toward Evan. It was the first time she'd considered that the freak accident might have ended her singing career. The flood and its aftermath had towered over her personal problems.

"You suppose there's any way we can take her to a doctor? My truck was up at her cabin, but that'll be gone now," Evan said.

"There's no road left to travel on. One of us could

try to walk out to telephone for help, but hard to tell how far we'd have to go. I figger there'll be people checkin' on this today or tomorrow. Better wait hit out, rather than for us to leave the women to fend for themselves. Ivy and me spent the night in that little barn." Ben motioned toward a little building high on the mountain. "Nothin' to eat, but at least hit was dry."

Late afternoon Ben heard the sound of an engine. A civil defense helicopter hovered over the area and Ben and Evan rushed out of the barn to wave their arms. The pilot signaled that he'd seen them and started to descend seeking a spot wide enough to land. He was more than a mile from the barn when he landed in a field swept level by the flood.

"Come on, Genna," Evan said. "Let's see if he'll take you to the doctor. I'm worried about you."

Genna didn't argue. She was getting worried herself; she couldn't make a sound now.

Evan recognized the pilot as a member of the National Guard. The man grabbed his hand. "Boy, is it good to see somebody alive. This whole creek is wiped out. For eight miles, I haven't seen a living soul or animal—nothing."

He willingly took Genna into the copter and since there was room for him, Evan went too. The man had brought a box of food that he left with Ben and Ivy.

"We'll be all right, so don't worry about us, Genna. Get yourself to a doctor," Ivy said.

Evan stayed with Genna all through the long examination. The doctor shook his head as a preface to his diagnosis.

"Frankly, I don't know what to tell you. Loss of voice might have come from the blow, or from the shock you'd had. At this point, all I can suggest is complete bed rest and no effort to talk at all. If you want to communicate, write on some paper."

Evan accompanied her into the hospital room before he left. She reached for the pad of paper the nurse had left and wrote, "I love you, Evan." He gathered her into his arms, tears in his eyes, and kissed her.

"I'll be back tomorrow. You'll be all right, sweetheart."

When he came the next day, his face was grave.

"I don't know if I should tell you this, but I know you're wondering. Mill Creek is a wasteland. Twenty people are missing or dead, and one of them is the missionary Miss Amelia."

Tears seeped from Genna's eyes. *Was she to have nothing of the past left*?

"The only good news is that your cabin is somehow still standing. The water went through and drenched everything and took the porch, but it seems as if the main wall of water didn't hit the house. You'll have a job on your hands, but I think it can be restored."

"Your mine?" She formed the words with her lips.

"Nothing left."

Within two weeks Genna's voice had returned slightly and the doctor allowed her to leave the hospital. A specialist had been called in from Johns Hopkins University School of Medicine for consultation.

"It may be, Miss Ross, that you can never sing again. At any rate, I would strongly advise you not to try for several months. After that, you can probably handle short engagements, but the long concert tours you used to take are probably a thing of the past."

The diagnosis was a blow to Genna, but perhaps this was God's answer. At least she would have the resort, she told herself with no particular comfort. She refused to let her mind dwell on the possibility that her career was ended.

The year was almost past and Genna sat on the reconstructed porch of her cabin. In spite of the worry over her voice and the postponement of their wedding, royalties from her book and a contract for the movie rights had brought in more money than she'd earned on concert tours. Michelle had spent several weeks with Genna and she was reconciled and eager for Genna and Evan to marry.

Evan had started an engineering consultant firm, and his first job had been on the resort hotel that had progressed on schedule. Due to open in a month, Genna had agreed to have her show billed on opening night, but here she sat afraid to open her mouth.

Many of the residents of the creek who'd survived the flood hadn't been able to handle the trauma of its aftermath. A few had sold their property to the resort company and moved away. Ben and Ivy had kept their land, but when they replaced their mobile home, they'd moved it to a high spot on the mountain far above the level the deluge had reached.

When Genna finally moved back into the cabin

after it was refurbished, she often left her bed during the night to peer out the window to see that her home wasn't threatened. When it rained at night, she didn't go to bed at all. But as the months passed, her worries had calmed and she felt that she was about back to normal, if she only had the courage to sing.

Evan was coming this evening so that they could make final plans for their wedding. Miss Amelia was gone, so she couldn't go there to calm her spirit. Changing into hiking shoes, she headed once again for Pinnacle Rock.

As she gazed out over the valley, she saw the few houses rebuilt since the flood. A tramway had been constructed from one mountain range to another and would be opened to the public next week. On the eastern mountain, she could see the tower of the ski lift soon to be open.

The hills hadn't changed. Mill Creek valley might be level as a floor, but the hills were still there. The land could be stripped for coal and reclaimed, resorts could be built, but the mountains remained. Yet she remembered the Psalmist's true source of strength:"My help comes from the Lord, the maker of heaven and earth."

Murmuring a prayer for courage, Genna opened her mouth and she sang, "Praise God from whom all blessings flow." Her voice seemed as strong as ever. Tears stung her eyes and slid over her cheeks. "God is so good," she murmured.

She wanted to share the good news with Evan as soon as possible, and she headed off the mountain. She saw him coming up the path and she began to sing. " 'He touched me, O, He touched me, and O, the joy that floods my soul.' "

Evan threw back his head and laughed exultantly. He drew her into his arms and swung her around as if she were a child.

"Am I to understand that you are practicing for the new Genna Ross Show?"

"That's right! My theme is going to be 'He Touched Me.' Can you think of anything more fitting?"

While she stood wrapped in his arms, Genna's thoughts quickly scanned the past fourteen years. She'd started out at this point in Evan's arms, and now she had come full circle. The way back had been a long one, full of frustration and disappointment, and many times her heartstrings had been stretched to the breaking point. If she and Evan had married when she was eighteen, what would her life have been like? Probably happy enough, but could the youthful Veevie ever have loved Evan as much as the mature Genna? Neither Genna nor Evan would ever doubt the power of a love that had persevered through the long years of separation.

Before Evan's lips claimed hers, the words of "One-Man Woman" came back to Genna with more poignancy than at any time in the past.

And now that he's opened his heart's closed
door,
I'll be a one-man woman forevermore.

A Letter To Our Readers

Dear Reader:

In order that we might better contribute to your reading enjoyment, we would appreciate your taking a few minutes to respond to the following questions and return to:

Karen Carroll, Editor
Heartsong Presents
P.O. Box 719
Uhrichsville, Ohio 44683

1. Did you enjoy reading *Heartstrings*?
   - ❑ Very much. I would like to see more books by this author!
   - ❑ Moderately
   - ❑ I would have enjoyed it more if

   ____

2. Where did you purchase this book? __________

   ____

3. What influenced your decision to purchase this book?
   - ❑ Cover
   - ❑ Back cover copy
   - ❑ Title
   - ❑ Friends
   - ❑ Publicity
   - ❑ Other __________

4. Please rate the following elements from 1 (poor) to 10 (superior).
   - ❑ Heroine ❑ Plot
   - ❑ Hero ❑ Inspirational theme
   - ❑ Setting ❑ Secondary characters

5. What settings would you like to see in Heartsong Presents Books?

   ____

   ____

6. What are some inspirational themes you would like to see treated in future books?

   ____

   ____

7. Would you be interested in reading other Heartsong Presents Books?
   - ❑ Very interested
   - ❑ Moderately interested
   - ❑ Not interested

8. Please indicate your age rage:
   - ❑ Under 18 ❑ 25-34 ❑ 46-55
   - ❑ 18-24 ❑ 35-45 ❑ Over 55

Name ______________________________________

Occupation ______________________________________

Address ______________________________________

City ________________ State ______ Zip ________